DAD'S GIRLFRIEND
and other
ANXIETIES

DAD'S GIRLFRIEND
and other
ANXIETIES

Kellye Crocker

Albert Whitman & Company
Chicago, Illinois

Library of Congress Cataloging-in-Publication data is on file with the publisher.

Text copyright © 2022 by Kellye Crocker
First published in the United States of America in 2022
by Albert Whitman & Company
ISBN 978-0-8075-1421-4 (hardcover)
ISBN 978-0-8075-1422-1 (ebook)

Printed in the United States of America
10 9 8 7 6 5 4 3 2 1 LB 26 25 24 23 22

Jacket art copyright © 2022 by Albert Whitman & Company
Jacket art by Simini Blocker
Design by Aphelandra

For more information about Albert Whitman & Company,
visit our website at www.albertwhitman.com.

For Mike,
whose heart is bigger
than a fourteener

CHAPTER 1

Ava should have been happy. She'd finished sixth grade an hour earlier and was eating a hot fudge sundae—her absolute favorite food—with her two very-besties, Kylie and Emma. She should have been happy, and she was. Just not *happy* happy.

Because: Colorado.

Obviously.

Ow. Ava pressed her hand to her forehead. Brain freeze. Who could blame her for wolfing it down? Shorty's served the perfect ratio of hot fudge to cold vanilla. Plus: Ava didn't want it to melt. The afternoon was a scorcher—way too hot and muggy, even for Iowa in early June. The girls had been lucky to snag an umbrella table on the crowded patio.

Ava wasn't going to worry about tomorrow. For now she was going to enjoy her sundae and listen to Emma complain about her big sister.

"She's into country music all of a sudden," Emma was saying, "and not good country—oh!—and she's started leaving her toothpaste spit in the sink."

"Ugh," Ava said.

"Gross," Kylie agreed.

"Right?" Emma looked at Ava. "How did your dad get a Colorado girlfriend anyway?"

Ava straightened. So much for not thinking about it. That was the question of the year. Dad worked at home but occasionally visited out-of-state suppliers. Somehow, he'd gone to Denver for work and ended up with a girlfriend.

"How does anyone get a girlfriend?" Ava raised her hands. "Amazon?"

It was a joke but it made as much sense as anything.

"Ha! Two-day delivery." Kylie took a bite of banana split. "Delish."

Emma waggled her spoon at Ava. "You always get the same thing," she grumbled, as if having a favorite sundae were a character flaw. Emma had ordered the "build your own," selecting caramel ice cream, blueberry topping, and corn chips.

"Ava knows what she likes," Kylie said. She stared at Emma a beat too long, as if sending a silent reminder that Ava was different now. If treated too roughly, she might crack like a glass doll.

These looks between them had started a month ago. After the horror show that was Field Day. After Dr. C. had diagnosed Ava with an anxiety disorder.

Ava was glad her friends cared about her, if that's what the looks meant. But their worries made Ava worry more.

"Was it a dating app?" Kylie stretched across the table to swipe one of Emma's chips.

"Why are you guys so interested?" Ava asked.

"Because it's interesting," Emma said. She dipped a chip into Ava's hot fudge.

"And romantic," Kylie said. "We've always known you with your dad."

Ava's fingers settled on her watch, which had belonged to her mother. "That's not changing." In the distance, three bicyclists followed a trail into the woods.

"It's kind of big news," Kylie said. "I heard the lunch ladies talking about it."

"You did?" Ava leaned forward. "What did they say?"

"That there are slim pickins around here for someone your dad's age. If you think about it, a lot of people are too old or too young or married already."

Ava hadn't thought about it. She and Dad lived in a small town surrounded by farms and smaller towns. Had he been lonely?

"They said they were glad he'd found someone," Kylie said.

"That makes it sound—"

"If they got married, you'd probably be in the wedding," she continued. "Maybe we could be in it with you?"

"Wait a minute."

"For your sake," Emma said, "I hope her daughter rinses her toothpaste spit."

"Holy guacamole," Ava whispered. "Do you think this is serious?"

"If it was a weekend trip, maybe not?" Kylie glanced at Emma, who nodded.

Ava shut her eyes for a moment. She still couldn't believe Dad was making her spend fourteen days with two strangers. In a state that overflowed with danger. Ava had started researching Colorado a week ago, as soon as she'd learned about their trip. She'd been so focused on safety, she hadn't considered the bigger picture. Was this relationship serious?

"Can we see her?" Kylie tapped her phone and slid it across the table. Because: Ava was the only human in the universe who didn't own a phone.

Ava found one of The Girlfriend's socials and pushed the phone back.

"Wow." Kylie looked up.

Ava's stomach dropped. "What?"

"She's hot."

Emma ran to Kylie's side of the table. "It's true," she confirmed. "Ava, your dad has a hot Colorado girlfriend."

"Stop," Ava moaned, covering her face with her hands. Other than The Girlfriend's long, honey-colored hair, she looked like most moms Ava knew.

"Oh, wow," Kylie said.

"What now?" Ava was already rounding the table.

Dad and The Girlfriend squished together on a boulder. Mountains, Colorado's most hazardous feature, hulked behind them. The Girlfriend's hand rested on Dad's knee. Dad's arm wrapped around her shoulders. She smiled at the camera. He smiled at her.

Emma took the phone. "My sister says if a guy likes three of your posts in a row, it means he wants to kiss you."

Ava wiped her palms on her shorts. "Did he do three?"

Emma shook her head.

Ava exhaled.

"I mean," Emma said, "he liked them all."

When did Dad have time for social media?

"Hey," Emma said. "Is this Mackenzie?"

Ava had never seen a picture of The Girlfriend's daughter, who also was twelve. "She's a reader too!" Dad had said, sounding like a hyper used-car salesman on TV. The girl in the picture wasn't reading, though. She was sitting—on nothing but air, one hand gripping a skateboard under her feet. Her long dark-purple hair stood straight up behind her helmet.

"That's amazing," Kylie said. "It has to be her, right?"

Emma gave Ava a playful shove. "You're going to have fun!"

Ava trudged back to her seat. Her remaining ice cream had softened, and the hot fudge had cooled. Emma, though, had barely touched hers. "Didn't you like it?" Ava asked.

"It was okay," Emma said, but she wrinkled her nose and shook her head no, which cracked them up.

It was a small win for Ava's hot fudge sundae. Shorty's was far away, and Emma had wasted her once-a-year visit on something new and strange. Sure, some people might think vanilla ice cream topped with hot fudge was basic. You know what else it was? Delicious. Ava's life was like a hot fudge sundae. Simple, sweet, and exactly as she liked it. If Dad was in love with someone in Colorado, that would ruin everything. Ava couldn't imagine it was true, but she intended to find out.

On most school days Ava rode the bus home. She usually found Dad bent over his laptop with Mouse snoozing at his feet. But the last day of school was special. The last day of *elementary school* was super special. Dad and Mouse were a two-member welcome-home party, waving and wagging from the driveway. It wasn't safe for them to stand there. Kylie's mom's van could hit them. In fact, Ava almost hoped it did—but only Dad. She didn't want him to get hurt. But if a gentle van bump sprained his ankle, say, maybe he'd cancel their trip tomorrow.

Kylie's mom eased alongside Dad with the precision of a pro racecar driver.

"Look at those sixth-grade graduates!" Dad peered into the van. "Hey, where's mine?"

Their tradition of celebrating the last day of school at Shorty's had started in kindergarten. So had Dad's goofy joke.

Kylie's mom got out to hug Dad. "Our little girls are growing up," she said.

She and Ava's mom had been friends since childhood. They had been thrilled to be pregnant at the same time. When Ava's mom died shortly after giving birth, Kylie's mom made sure to arrange regular play dates—to give Dad a break, but also to spend time with her best friend's daughter. Ava and Kylie's friendship had grown as they did. They were proud second-gen BFFs.

Ava grabbed her backpack. "I'll call you as soon as I get home," she said.

If she didn't get struck by lightning. Or eaten by a bear. Or sick from the too-thin air.

"You'll be okay," Kylie said.

Mouse barked and danced as if Ava had been gone forever.

"Poor guy," Dad said. "He was confused when you didn't get off the bus."

As Ava headed toward the house, she turned one last time to wave goodbye.

"Have fun!" Emma shouted.

Ava dropped her backpack in the entryway and hugged Mouse.

"How was your last day?" Dad asked.

"Fine." Her heart raced. She had to ask. Ava straightened and took a breath. "Um…Dad? Is it serious with you and"—she could not say "The Girlfriend"—"you and Jenn?"

"What do you mean?" His pale cheeks went pink.

"You know." This was so embarrassing.

"You're my number one, Ava, and always will be. You know that, right? I think you'll really like Jenn and Mackenzie." Dad tapped her arm. "Come help with the salad."

He hadn't really answered her question. Had he dodged it on purpose? Maybe Ava could ask him again later. For now, it seemed best to move on.

"Why can't I stay with Mrs. Mendez or Grandmom?" she asked, trailing him into the kitchen.

Ava loved visiting her grandparents and Uncle Steve—her mom's parents and brother—at their organic dairy farm a short drive away. But when Dad traveled during the school year, Ava and Mouse stayed with Mrs. Mendez. The school bus stopped right in front of her house across the street, and Grandmom was allergic to dogs.

"This feels so sudden," Ava added. Since she'd started seeing Dr. C., Ava had learned she didn't do well with change and needed extra time for transitions.

Dad sighed. "You've had a whole week to think about it."

A pile of bright-green lettuce leaves sat on the counter. Ava picked up a handful and ran it under the tap. Her stomach hurt. Did she have food poisoning? Could hot fudge go bad?

"Remember what Dr. C. said? Too much time isn't good, either." Dad peeled a carrot. "And what about avoiding stressful situations? What did she say about that, Baby Ava Girl?"

Now Ava sighed. "It makes them worse," she mumbled.

"That's right." He turned to look at her. "Traveling, meeting people—those are all a part of life. Colorado is beautiful. It'll be good for you to see more of the country."

Ava didn't want to see more. She wanted to stay home where she belonged, with her dog, her friends, and her family. This was a truth as strong as gravity.

Spongy bits of black soil clung to the lettuce. This morning, it had been growing happily in the backyard.

"Did you know cute little ground squirrels can kill you?" Ava had uncovered this horrifying fact during her class's last media center session.

Dad stopped mid-slice into the carrot. "What?"

"They can give you plague, Dad. You have a fifty-fifty chance of dying. Well, if you don't go to the doctor—but, still."

Dad set down his knife. "What are you talking about?"

"Colorado!" Wasn't he listening? "It's super dangerous!"

"I'd never put you in danger, Ava." He frowned. "Wait—have you been trying to find dangerous things in Colorado?"

If she had, it wouldn't have been difficult. "I've been learning about it."

It wasn't Ava's fault the state was so terrible.

Dad removed his glasses and pinched the bridge of his nose. "All places have dangers."

"But the mountains are bad—they're like magnets for danger," Ava said. "Even Denver—it doesn't have mountains, but the air is too thin. Did you know it's called the Mile High City? You can get sick—"

"Stop."

"And die. The *air* can kill you, Dad."

Dad returned his glasses to his face. "Ava, are you feeling anxious?"

The question put her whole self on red alert. Dr. C. had said it was important for Ava to learn to identify her feelings and name them. But she talked about feelings like they were Legos, easy to recognize and sort by size, shape, and color. Ava's feelings were like Dad's Mystery Soup—a bubbling mishmash.

"How about some belly breathing?" Dad asked. Since learning the relaxation technique, he thought it was the answer to everything.

"I don't need belly breathing." Ava stomped her foot. "I just need to stay home!"

VERY IMPORTANT NOTEBOOK
Property of: Ava Louise Headly

Belly Breathing

1. Place a hand on your belly.
2. Inhale slowly through your nose, imagining that your belly is a balloon filling with air.
3. Hold breath 2 seconds.
4. Exhale slowly.
5. Hold 2 seconds.
6. Repeat.

CHAPTER 2

The best day of summer vacation was the first day. But instead of letting Ava enjoy her freedom, Dad had jostled her awake before sunrise so they could drive two hours to the airport to catch their plane to horrible Colorado. Now, as they were about to land, Ava felt strange—hot but cold. A bit tingly. Somewhat buzzy.

This trip made no sense. This was *Dad*. Practical, responsible, and sort of boring. Dad, whose idea of a good time was catching a catfish bigger than Uncle Steve's. The thought of him falling in love, especially with some Colorado Girlfriend, seemed about as likely as him running away to join the circus.

Which was to say, never in a million bitrillion years.

Even if she was hot.

Dad tapped Ava's arm and motioned across their row of seats. "See the mountains?"

Large adults blocked her view, which was fine. Fortunately, The Girlfriend lived in Denver, which was mountain-free. Of course, cities had crime, smog, and drivers with road rage, so they weren't safe, either. It was unfair how a parent could force a kid to go somewhere against her will. It was kidnapping, practically.

"You know you can't shun me forever, right?" Dad's voice was playful.

Ava twisted away, toward the snoring stranger in the window seat. In her research, she'd found many pictures of "Welcome to colorful Colorado" signs. But now, through the plastic oval window, Colorado looked like a bunch of brown and tan rectangles. Flat rectangles, the same colors as the welcome signs. Ava couldn't help comparing the sad view to Iowa's gently rolling hills splashed with every shade of green.

"I wish you'd talk to me, Baby Ava Girl. This is going to be fun."

The thing was, Dad usually was careful. He reminded Ava to wear her bike helmet, use sunscreen, and never share personal information on the internet. He even insisted she sit to eat a lollipop. Why risk their lives to introduce her to The Girlfriend and her daughter?

Hello, Mackenzie. It's very nice to meet you, Ava practiced in her head. Soon she'd have to say it for real. She wasn't used to meeting people. She and Kylie had been friends since before they could eat solid food. They'd met Emma in kindergarten.

The internet had been less helpful than usual too. Ava had perked up when she found an article about how to get a twelve-year-old girl to like you. But it had been about dating. "Keep your nails clipped and clean," the article advised. "Girls don't like untidy boys." Even if she'd wanted to date a twelve-year-old girl (and Ava thought she was too young for dating), the article sounded like it was written in the pioneer days.

What are your hobbies and interests, Mackenzie?

The best tips had come from articles about making a good impression in a job interview. "Be your sweet Ava self," Mrs. Mendez had said when Ava had dropped off Mouse. But it had been eons since Mrs. Mendez had been twelve. To make regular friends, those who hadn't known her forever, Ava had to be more than her small-town self—and hide her anxiety.

The plane interrupted her thoughts with an alarming mechanical screech. A lurch and a rumble followed, as if the plane had dropped its guts. Ava stiffened and scanned for trouble. Just the other day, *The Des Moines Register* had reported that a goose had flown into a plane and almost caused a crash. Dad had hustled her out the door so fast that morning, Ava had left her newspaper. Of course, if she had a phone, she could have read the news online.

The point was: Plane crashes were rare. Still, one goose was all it took.

Ava's fingers found her watch. The hands were stuck at some long-ago 4:15. Granddad, her mom's dad, had added holes to the leather band so it wouldn't slip off Ava's wrist. Even though the watch didn't work, it was her favorite possession.

She imagined it sent her mom a secret signal, like Batman's. Maybe it was a flash of lightning, a heavenly email, or a Queen Latifah song. (Ava's mom was way into women rappers in high school, according to Kylie's mom.) Whatever the signal, Ava's mom would know her daughter needed help, so she'd shoot some extra love down to Earth.

But Ava didn't touch her watch only when she needed mystical help. She touched it to say, "I never really knew you, but I love you" and to wish her mom a happy birthday or Mother's Day. She touched it before a test and to fight the awful and ordinary missingness—the empty space where her mom should have been. Sometimes she touched it for no reason. Today, though, Ava needed all the help she could get.

―――――――――

The Denver airport's steep, towering escalator made Ava's knees tremble, and she gripped the rubber rails. Her heavy backpack messed with her balance, and Ava scrunched her toes inside her sandals. She always was careful after reading about a woman who'd lost a pinkie toe when it got caught in an escalator's sharp metal teeth.

The escalator deposited them into a bright, bustling terminal. A sleek white train—nothing like the Iowa trains that backed up Main Street with endless ka-chunking cars—whisked them to another part of the terminal, where they rode another soaring escalator.

"Look." Dad nodded at a sign. "Welcome to Denver," it said against a snowcapped mountain and brilliant blue sky, the image reflected in a lake as clear and smooth as a mirror.

Ava frowned. The picture was false advertising and hazardous for visitors who weren't careful about research. One little misstep in the mountains and—too bad—you were dead.

Ava imagined herself in a casket, golden curls tumbling over a little pillow. (In real life, her hair was wavy and short.) A young life ended by an innocent-looking Colorado ground squirrel. Dad shook his fists, howling, "I shouldn't have made her go to Denver!"

What he said for real: "There she is!"

Except: He didn't say the words as much as sing them.

Ava chased him around a metal gate into the waiting area and stopped. Dad dropped their bags and swept a tall woman into his arms. Where was her daughter? When their hug ended, Ava started toward them, but—no.

Just.

No.

Ava halted, shut her eyes, and spun around. Too late. The image of Dad kissing The Girlfriend had burned her eyeballs. It's not that she thought kissing was bad. She just hadn't thought much about it at all, especially about Dad—of all people!—doing it.

"Ava," he called, waving, as if remembering he had a daughter. "This is Jenn." Had he been using one of those teeth whiteners?

The lips that had smushed against Dad's smiled at Ava. "I'm so happy to finally meet you," The Girlfriend said. "Can I give you a hug?"

Ava nodded, her cheeks warm. The Girlfriend smelled nice, sort of like cinnamon candy.

"Mackenzie's around here somewhere." She looked behind her, as if her daughter were hiding in a potted plant.

For all The Girlfriend knew, Mackenzie could have been snatched by kidnappers, forced onto a plane, and transported to a criminal lair. Or, she could have tripped, hit her head, and had amnesia. What if bullies had her cornered in the ladies' room?

The Girlfriend pulled her phone from her bag. "I'll text her."

Ava glared at Dad, shouting with her eyes: MACKENZIE HAS HER OWN PHONE! Plus: SHE MIGHT HAVE BEEN KID-NAPPED! But the only thing Dad's eyeballs cared about was The Girlfriend.

A commotion in the distance caught Ava's attention.

"'Scuse me, sorry, coming through!" The girl from the picture, long purple hair flying, silver-sequined tennis shoes flashing, careened through the crowd. Dodging people and luggage, she hurdled over a service dog. If she'd been a car, her brakes would have screeched when she stopped in front of The Girlfriend.

"Careful," The Girlfriend said. "You almost plowed me over."

Ava was small for her age. Mackenzie looked like she came from pro basketball players.

"You can't run off like that," The Girlfriend said.

"I told you I wanted to check—real quick—if Tattered Cover had *Zorn Mutiny: Escape to Kleptar*." Breathless, Mackenzie raised a bag as if it were an Olympic medal. "I've been trying to find it for-ev-er!"

Hello, Mackenzie, Ava silently practiced. What are your interests? That wasn't right…what was it? Ack! She'd forgotten hobbies!

"You were supposed to be here to welcome Eric and Ava," The Girlfriend said.

Hobbies and interests. Hobbies and interests.

"Sorry." Mackenzie turned slightly, her dark eyes falling on Ava. "Welcome."

Ava didn't know what to say. Thank you? "Hello" suddenly seemed too formal.

"You were on your phone." Mackenzie turned back to her mother. "I didn't run off."

"You're being rude," The Girlfriend said in a loud whisper.

The Girlfriend and her daughter shared the same body type—fit—and they both had brown eyes. But Mackenzie's skin was golden brown and her eyebrows were dark. The Girlfriend's skin and hair were light.

"Can't I even—" Mackenzie said.

"We'll talk about it later."

"You're accusing—"

"Later." The Girlfriend turned to Dad and Ava. "I'm sorry."

"No worries. Good to see you again, Mackenzie." Dad nudged Ava forward. "This is my daughter, Ava. Ava, can you say hi?" He sounded singsongy, as if he were talking to a baby.

"Hi, Mackenzie," Ava said, instantly regretting it. Because: She wanted to cooperate with Dad as little as possible.

"Z," Mackenzie said.

Ava's stomach clenched. Was that something cool Colorado kids said to each other?

Dad ho-ho-hoed like a weird Santa. "That's right." He turned to Ava. "Mackenzie goes by Z now."

Ava nodded, hoping her heartbeat would return to normal soon. How could Dad have told her the wrong name?

COLORADO DANGERS
(extremely partial list)

Air: Altitude sickness can be <u>fatal</u>.

Wildlife: Bears, mountain lions, mountain goats, bighorn sheep, moose, elk, rattlesnakes

Thunderstorms: Lightning (a top state for lightning deaths), flash floods, mudslides, high-elevation tornadoes

Falling: Rocks, trees, people

Creepy Crawlies: Spiders and ticks can make you sick or hurt you with painful bites. Parasites can slip into your guts if you drink bad water from lakes, streams, and rivers (or swallow some while swimming). Infected fleas pass bubonic plague to rodents—<u>especially adorable ground squirrels</u>—and they can give it to people. Fatal half the time (if you don't see a doctor).

WHY WOULD ANYONE VISIT COLORADO???

CHAPTER 3

The airport parking garage was a maze with sharp turns The Girlfriend took too fast in her cherry-red Jeep. Plus: Dad's chatter and gleaming teeth created driver distractions.

As they left the airport, Dad turned in his seat. "Look, Ava, the mountains."

Shadowy humps huddled under silver clouds in the distance. They looked nothing like their pictures. A barren field—not a fairy-tale mirror lake—dominated the view.

"You talk," Z said, "right?"

Ava turned. She hated when people commented on how quiet she was. Like there was a law about how much a person should talk, and they were the Talking Police ready to haul her to Quiet Jail.

"You've only said two words," Z said.

"Oh."

"Three."

In the front, their parents murmured, a constant, urgent-sounding drone.

"I talk." A familiar heat returned to Ava's cheeks. What a dumb thing to say!

Z stretched purple gum out of her mouth and swung it around her finger, as if she knew nothing about germs. "Your dad's nice."

Ava nodded. Did nodding count? She cleared her throat. "Yeah. He is." It didn't contribute much but it got her word count up. After one of Dad's visits to Denver, he'd mentioned meeting Z. How much time had they spent together? How well did they know each other?

"I live with my mom, but I see my dad as much as possible." The sequins on Z's tennis shoes flashed as she jiggled one foot. "He travels a lot."

"Your mom seems nice."

Why, oh, why hadn't Ava said this at first, when Z had said her dad was nice? That was the frustrating thing about talking. You had to say the right thing at the right time. But while you figured that out, the person had said another thing. Conversations were exhausting.

"Have you?" Z strained against her seat belt. "Heard of him?"

What was she talking about?

"It doesn't matter." Z waved a hand. "He's famous is all. He's on that show, *Make Me a Top Model*? He's the photographer and a judge."

Ava nodded. Z was talking about her dad. Ava had heard of the show but hadn't seen it.

The mountains had disappeared. A cluster of skyscrapers rose nearby. Cars, buses, and bicycles clogged the streets.

"He travels all over the world," Z continued, "and shoots for all the big magazines."

The only famous person Ava had met was the artist who carved a cow out of butter at the Iowa State Fair.

"He always brings me presents, even though I say, 'Rodrigo, stop! You're spoiling me!'"

Did Z call her dad by his first name because he was famous? Or was that a Colorado thing? The thought of Ava saying, "Hey, Eric, how's it going?" seemed laughable—embarrassing, even, like seeing Dad in his underwear.

Z fished a phone from her pocket and tossed it to Ava, who, unprepared, nearly fumbled it. Even in its protective case, the phone looked thin and fancy. When Emma and Kylie had gotten phones this past school year, Ava begged Dad for one too. He said she was too young.

"It's nice." Ava placed the phone beside Z.

"He got it in Tokyo." Only one of Z's shoulders lifted in a small, off-balance shrug. "They cost more here. A lot a lot more."

They passed a park busy with walkers, runners, and bikers. Narrow, curving streets held a hodgepodge of shops and restaurants in old, redbrick buildings.

"Your dad sounds cool," Ava said.

"He's the best." Z thumbed her phone and handed it back to Ava. "That's him."

A moody portrait of a man filled the screen. He had brown skin, spiky salt-and-pepper hair, and tattoos. Iowa fathers didn't look like this—young and old at the same time, handsome and ugly, safe and dangerous. Ava thought of Dad's glasses and plain haircut, his freckled white skin. "Rodrigo looks like a rock star," she said.

"Exactly. I can't wait for you to meet him."

"Yeah," Ava said, although this was a surprise. Z's parents were divorced, but maybe they were friends?

Z and The Girlfriend lived in a town house, a skinny, two-story "unit" stuck to two other units. The garage was separate from the house, but its back door opened to a small, fenced patio behind the town house. "Behold the backyard," The Girlfriend said with a little laugh.

Ava tried to keep the shock off her face. Compared to her sweeping lawn with the tree fort and deck her dad and Uncle Steve had built, this "yard" hardly seemed worthy of the name. A small, concrete slab held—barely—a grill, a small table with a yellow umbrella, and four chairs with matching cushions. There wasn't a blade of grass, only a few droopy flowers poking through the cracked dirt that bordered the garage. Mouse would have hated it.

Inside, the house's lower level was mostly one open rectangle, with areas for eating, cooking, and watching TV. At least the bathroom had a door that closed.

Z kicked off her shoes. "Let's go to my room," she said.

"Wait!" The Girlfriend grabbed a water bottle from a cabinet, filled it, and crossed the room. "It's so dry here," she said, handing it to Ava. "It's important to stay hydrated."

"Thanks," Ava said. She'd learned that people in Colorado lose water through breathing twice as quickly as people at sea level, thanks to the dangerously dry air and high elevation.

"Yeah, thanks, Mom." Z raised and dropped her hands.

"Since you live here, Mackenzie, I'm confident you can get your own water."

"Z."

"Z," The Girlfriend repeated with a sigh. "Sorry."

"Why can't you remember, though?"

"Because I'm old." The Girlfriend laughed, sharing a quick look with Dad before turning back. "I said I'm sorry." She lowered her voice. "Do we need to have a chat?"

Z ran a big toe along a crack in the wooden floor. "No."

"Great." The Girlfriend smiled—her teeth were white too. "Before you two run off, why don't we get to know each other a little?"

"Great idea," Dad said.

Ava's stomach knotted. It felt as if The Girlfriend had pulled out a pop quiz. Plus: It seemed like Dad would have said "great idea" even if she'd suggested murdering baby bunnies.

"I'm so happy to finally meet you, Ava," The Girlfriend said, patting the sofa cushion beside her. "Sit here."

Dad sat on The Girlfriend's other side. In fact, he sat too close, invading her space.

"She doesn't talk much," Z said.

A flash of alarm zipped through Ava. It was the Jeep conversation again, but now Dad and The Girlfriend were in on it, their eyes like burning spotlights.

"I talk," Ava said.

"Z, that's not polite," The Girlfriend said.

"What?" Z sprawled in an upholstered chair, dangling her giraffe legs over one arm.

"Ava's a little shy," Dad said, as if she weren't right there. "She'll warm up."

Ava wished the sofa had a trap door that could swallow her—or Dad.

"Don't pressure her," The Girlfriend said, giving Z a look.

The knot in Ava's stomach pulled tighter. Did they know about what happened at Field Day?

"Why is that not polite?" Z asked.

"I talk," Ava repeated, too loud.

"But not that much," Z said, "right?"

"Your dad says you do so well in school, Ava," The Girlfriend said. "And you're going to middle school in the fall? That's exciting."

"Scary" would be more accurate, and it was a junior/senior high, but Ava nodded. Emma and Kylie were excited to go to the big school farther away. Kids from four counties went there for grades seven through twelve. But Ava didn't like change—especially when it involved older teenagers who might enjoy bullying younger kids.

"Didn't you just finish sixth grade?" Z asked. She swung her legs high over the back of the chair and leaned back, upside down.

"Yeah," Ava said.

"Me too," Z said. "That's middle school, though."

How could Z talk with all the blood rushing to her head?

"Different places do it differently," Dad said.

His hand cupped The Girlfriend's bare knee. Did she like that?

"Um, Jenn?" Ava's heart drummed. "What are your hobbies and interests?"

"I'm sorry?" The Girlfriend leaned closer.

"She wants to know if you have hobbies," Z shouted.

Ava's cheeks were a five-alarm fire now. Her lungs didn't have enough air, which wasn't surprising in the Mile High City. But what if…what if Field Day happened again? Here? Now? She pushed the terrible thought away. She breathed.

"And interests." Ava's voice came out a whisper. "Hobbies and interests."

The Girlfriend smiled. "I do, Ava. Thank you for asking. Let's see…I like to read—I hear you do too—and play board games. I like running and hiking. Do you like being outdoors?"

"Kind of."

"You like going to the state park with Mouse," Dad said, butting in.

"You have a mouse?" Z asked. Seriously, how could she stay upside down so long?

"That's my dog," Ava said. She looked at Dad. If he hadn't told them about Mouse, this relationship wasn't serious.

"I wish I had a dog," Z said. "And a snake. Is your dog small like a mouse?"

"A snake?" Ava said.

"You can't cuddle a snake," The Girlfriend said. "And some live thirty years."

"Well, obviously, I'd take it with me when I go to college," Z said. "Sixth grade is part of elementary where you live?"

Ava hadn't had a chance to answer Z's question about Mouse's size before she'd asked about school. On top of that, Z was talking with her mom. Upside down. "Yeah," Ava said. "Seventh and eighth are junior high."

"There are a lot of changes in middle school." Z's upside-down face was red and serious. "A lot a lot of changes. Like lockers, and no recess, and some teachers are mean."

"Z," The Girlfriend's voice carried a warning. "Ava will be fine."

"She's a great student," Dad said, which wasn't the point.

"I'm warning her is all." Z finally pulled herself upright and spun around to sit the normal way. "You might not have any classes with your friends—or even lunch," she told Ava. "You might be all alone."

Z's warnings had worked. Ava was even more worried about junior high. But that wouldn't matter if she didn't survive Colorado.

CHAPTER 4

Ava ran up the stairs at her grandparents' farmhouse all the time, but the short climb to Z's room left her winded. Her heavy backpack hadn't helped.

"It's the altitude," Z said.

Ava rubbed her arms. High altitude could make people sick. It could kill them.

Z opened the first door in the hall. Bursts of blue, purple, pink, and gold swept across the ceiling, walls, and even the wooden floor. Plus: orange and yellow. And green. The more Ava looked, the more colors appeared.

"This is your room?" Ava immediately regretted her words. But instead of pointing out how obvious the answer was, Z grinned, one corner of her mouth higher than the other.

"It's a nebula," she said, waving, "a space cloud."

White paper stars hung from the ceiling with dozens of tiny

white party lights. "It's so pretty," Ava said, tiptoeing around clothes, books, and action figures.

A high platform rose next to the wall on four thick posts. Was Z's *bed* up there? Shimmering curtains spilled off the sides to the floor. Z flipped one back with a flourish, revealing a recliner, a beanbag chair, a lamp, a bookshelf, some art supplies, and a skateboard.

"Holy guacamole," Ava whispered. In her room, the walls were white. Her twin bed sat on the floor. There was no secret hideout.

Z pulled out her phone and bouncy music played. "Another Rodrigo present." She nodded at the wireless speakers. "You want to see some of his pictures?"

She zipped over to a stool at a purple-painted desk. Two framed prints hung above it. They read, "Love you to the moon and back" and "We are all made of stars."

"You must really like space," Ava said.

"Well, yeah. Most astronauts do."

"You want to be an astronaut? You'd ride in a rocket?"

Z looked up from her laptop. "Wouldn't you?"

Was she kidding? "What if something went wrong?"

"They teach you what to do." Z spun on her stool, kicking out her long legs, and Ava jumped back.

As Z returned to her laptop, Ava wanted to say: But what if something horrible happened, something no one expected? She wanted to say: That was the problem with awful surprises—you did not, could not, see them coming. All you could do was prepare as well as possible and hope to deal with what came. And she really wanted to say: Most important? Never, ever put yourself in risky situations.

"Lookit." Z made room for Ava to sit beside her. "They're in Antarctica. Rodrigo had to shoot fast."

The models looked bored, posing on pristine snow with still blue water in the foreground. They wore tiny bikinis and fur boots. Looking at it, Ava felt cold—and mad. The photo seemed sexist and silly, not to mention dangerous for the models.

"So, you don't want to be an astronaut," Z said. "What do you want to be when you grow up? A farmer? Is pretty much everyone a farmer in Iowa?"

"My dad isn't. Lots of people aren't."

Ava touched her watch. She'd heard the family story often: After graduating from Iowa State, her parents married and moved into what Grandmom called "the little house on the dairy." Ava's mom had adored her cows, naming each after a favorite woman author, and had long dreamed of running her parents' farm. After she died, Dad and baby Ava moved to town and Uncle Steve took the house. Ava still visited the farm often.

She was popular with the herd for her head scratches—right behind the poll, the pointy place between the cows' ears. Bits of dirt and hay collected there, where the girls couldn't reach, and they'd lower and angle their heads until Ava's fingers found just the right spot. She loved them too, but she didn't want to be a farmer. Ava wasn't sure how to explain any of this to Z.

"Look." The models, in different bikinis, threw snowballs. Z rocked their shared stool. "I can't wait for you to meet him."

"Is he coming here?"

"He can't." In the next photo, the models sipped from steaming mugs. It was so fake. Iowans knew brutal cold. Nobody was stupid enough to go out nearly naked.

Z clicked a video of the shoot. "He's meeting us in the mountains," she said.

A tingle zipped from Ava's armpits down her sides.

He's meeting us in the mountains.

She understood the meaning of those words, together, in that order.

But it was as if Z were speaking another language. Either Ava had misunderstood or Z was wrong. Ava wasn't going to the mountains, horrible Colorado's most dangerous region.

"What do you mean?" she said.

They stared at each other.

"We're going Monday," Z said. As if that cleared up everything, she turned back to the screen. When Ava didn't reply, Z said, "Eric got a cabin—one of the really good ones. It's going to be super a-ma-zing because Rodrigo will be up there for a shoot! You'll love him, everybody does." She frowned. "Wait. You really didn't know?"

Ava exhaled and shook her head.

"The mountains are a-*ma*-zing!"

This couldn't be right. Ava had given Dad loads of evidence proving beyond a reasonable doubt that Colorado's mountains were seriously life-threatening. Plus: She'd told him how much she, personally, didn't want to visit them. Ever. Despite this, and even though he claimed to love her more than anything, Ava's father had rented a cabin in the mountains.

It might as well have been Mars, which Z, no doubt, would have liked too.

As awful as that was—and it was awful to infinity times infinity—it was far, far worse that Dad had hidden his plan. His deception felt like a kazillion needles stabbing Ava's heart.

"Maybe Eric wanted it to be a surprise?"

"Yeah." Ava stroked her watch. "Hey, is there a bathroom up here?" She needed a moment—and she didn't want to go downstairs for obvious Dad-related reasons.

"My mom's room." Z clicked on another photo. "Down the hall."

"You're probably right, about Dad wanting to surprise me. Don't tell him, okay?"

Ava would plan her own surprise—one that kept them in Denver.

Ava dropped onto the closed toilet seat, shut her eyes, and covered her ears. She took slow, deep breaths. She wished she could see Kylie and Emma. "What your dad did? That's really messed up," Emma would say. Kylie would nod sympathetically and give Ava a hug.

Was he in love? Did he love The Girlfriend more than Ava? What was it about her that would make Dad rent a secret mountain cabin?

After more breathing, Ava stood and washed her hands. The yellow hand towel matched the delicate flowers on the wallpaper. Ava helped herself to a pump of lotion. It smelled like Granddad's lemon bars. She and Dad didn't have lotion or fluffy towels.

The pale hair on Ava's arms rose. Did she and Dad have white walls and flat towels—had she never thought of painting her desk—because Ava didn't have a mom? If that were true, what other important stuff was she missing?

Suddenly, everything around her looked womanly and mysterious.

Ava picked up a perfume bottle and removed the stopper. It was the same spicy-sweet scent she'd noticed when The Girlfriend had hugged her. Ava dabbed it behind both ears, like the fancy women in the black-and-white movies she and Mrs. Mendez binged.

Next, she studied the array of hair products. Ava hated her wavy hair. It wasn't straight or curly, and it always flipped the wrong way. It was so short, most of her ears showed, and Dad wouldn't let her get them pierced.

After hearing horror stories about tangles, tears, and tantrums, Dad had kept Ava's hair short when she was little. As she grew older, she imagined long hair getting caught in fans, carnival rides, and garbage disposals. Short hair had seemed best. But was it?

Impulsively, Ava spritzed Big 'N Bouncy Curl Boost onto her head. It had a chemical smell and stung her scalp. She styled her hair with her fingers. But it didn't make her hair big or bouncy or curly. It was flat, wet, and sticky. Everyone would wonder what had happened. The Girlfriend might get mad Ava had used her stuff.

Panic rising, Ava scrubbed hand soap into her hair. She bent over the sink and rinsed, sputtering as water snaked into her nose. She reached for the hand towel and mashed it to her head. As she pulled it away, Ava glimpsed herself in the mirror. With her light-colored hair stuck to her scalp, she looked bald! Her shirt was wet. Water pooled around the sink and spilled to the floor like a waterfall.

Ava hurried to the closet next to the bathtub and was relieved to find towels. She didn't want to use The Girlfriend's good ones, so, straining on tiptoe, she reached all the way to the back. As Ava pulled one out, a sandwich bag fell to the floor. It held three plastic sticks that looked somewhat like markers. Someone had written a date on each: April 5, April 8, April 9. Two months ago. She removed one from the bag. On the side was a little window that held a plus sign. Ava peered closer. Tiny words lined up beside the window:

Pregnant +

Not Pregnant –

Holy guacamole.

A plus sign meant pregnant.

Heart thudding, Ava pulled out the other sticks, accidentally dropping one. It also had a plus. The third stick had one all-capital-letter word: **PREGNANT**.

Two pluses and a **PREGNANT**.

The Girlfriend was going to have a baby.

An invisible shard of ice—razor-sharp, bone-chilling, heart-stopping—pierced Ava's chest.

Were Dad and The Girlfriend going to have a baby?

A relationship couldn't get more serious than that.

Ava leaned against the closet, steadying herself. She was too young to have a heart attack. But with the Mile High City's too-thin air, maybe it was possible.

They hadn't known each other long.

Would Dad…

No.

They were strangers, practically. They didn't even know about Mouse.

Would Dad and The Girlfriend…

No!

Would Dad and The Girlfriend get married, like Kylie had said?

NO! NO! NO!

Known Facts about The Girlfriend:

- Lives in Denver, Colorado
- Z's mom
- Kisses Dad
- Smells good
- Lets Z Have a Cell Phone
- Doesn't worry when Z is missing
- Drives too fast
- Friends with ex-husband?
- Hobbies and Interests: reading, board games, running, hikes, outdoors
- Brilliant decorator
- GOING TO HAVE A BABY!?!?!?!?

CHAPTER 5

How and when Ava had come to sit on the bathroom floor was a mystery. She rose shakily and wiped up the water she'd spilled. She was tempted to hide the towel in the closet, but if you weren't careful, mold and mildew could sprout and cause health problems. Instead, she spread it along the side of the tub to dry. Finally, Ava returned the sticks to their hiding place and scanned the bathroom one last time.

"Ava?" Z pounded the door. "Are you in there?"

"Hey." Ava tried to sound casual as she opened the door. What if Z thought she'd been pooping this whole time or that she was a weirdo who took random baths in people's tubs?

"You were gone so—yowza! What did you do?"

"Nothing." Ava wiped her hands on her shorts.

"Did you…" Z fingered Ava's hair. "Put something in your hair?"

"No." Ava stepped back. "Stop."

Z's hand dropped. "Were you trying a new look?"

Ava sighed. "Your mom has a lot of products."

Z brightened. "If you dyed your hair, it'd look 100 percent better." She dashed past Ava to the cabinet under the sink and dug through the cluttered bottom drawer.

"I think we—yay!" Z waved two squished tubes. "Pink or green?"

"I don't know." Ava rubbed the back of her head, her fingers discovering a crunchy clump. "My dad might not like it."

Z smiled her lopsided smile. "It's your hair," she said, which was an excellent point.

Also: Maybe Ava's plain hair would look sort of cool pink or green.

"It washes out," Z said. "I mean, after a while. I'll get a towel."

"Wait!"

Z halted.

"Um…" What if Z found the sticks? If she didn't know her mom was pregnant, Ava didn't want her finding out now. She needed to figure out if this involved Dad and her first. "Is the dye safe?"

"What?"

"The chemicals." Ava swallowed.

"It's fine." Z turned toward the closet.

"But what about the…" Ava was desperate. "FDA?"

Z turned again. "The FD—what?"

"The Food and Drug Administration—do they say it's safe? What about the Environmental Working Group?" Ava had often checked the organization's website. "Are they tested on animals?"

"You know what?" Z walked back, dropped the tubes into the drawer, and nudged it shut with her foot. "Never mind."

A fist tightened in Ava's chest. She'd wanted to try it, sort of.

Z crossed her arms and studied Ava. "You're kind of a scaredy-cat, aren't you?" she said, then hurried away.

Of all the insults Z could have chosen, that was the worst.

Because it was true.

Maybe Z knew about her anxiety and was throwing it in her face? Maybe Z didn't know, but sensed—as Ava did—that something was wrong deep inside her.

Ava didn't want to return to Z's super-cool bedroom. But what was she supposed to do? Go downstairs and hang with her back-stabbing, cabin-renting Dad and his stick-hiding, baby-having Girlfriend? Ava walked into Z's room as if it were a normal thing to do.

Z's fingers clacked on the keyboard. She popped her gum. She didn't look up.

The Colorado air stretched extra thin between them.

Ava hefted her backpack from the floor and walked to Z's under-bed hideout. She pulled aside the curtain and braced for Z to tell her that only cool-haired people were allowed. But Z's typing was the only sound. Even Rodrigo's speakers were silent.

Ava retrieved her notebook and pen from her backpack and burrowed into Z's beanbag chair. Dr. C. had encouraged her to write about worries—she called it journaling—and said scientists had found it helped people feel better.

Dad was secretly forcing her to go to the mountains. The Girlfriend was pregnant. Z thought she was a scaredy-cat. It was only her first day in Colorado!

What if The Girlfriend and Rodrigo weren't only divorced friends? What if they wanted to get back together and have another baby? That wouldn't explain why Dad and Ava were here, though. It was so confusing. But grownups did confusing things sometimes.

The curtain parted, and Z stepped inside. "What are you writing?"

Ava angled her arm so Z couldn't see. "Nothing," she said, as her pen flew across the page. Ava considered herself a kind person—usually. "Scaredy-cat" still stung.

Z sprawled in her recliner. After a quiet moment, Ava peeked at her. Z was engrossed in her new Zorn book, a long leg thrown over one of the chair's arms.

Exhausted from writing, Ava returned her supplies to the backpack and pulled out one of her comfort reads, *Charlotte's Web*. If she focused on the words, she could escape for a while.

The girls read silently, apart but together, for a long time.

"Salutations." Z sat upright now, her book and phone at her feet. "Salutations" was what Charlotte, the book's namesake spider, had said when she met Wilbur the pig. It was, she told him, a fancy way of saying "hello" or "good morning."

"Salutations," Ava said.

"Have you read it before?" Z asked.

"Lots of times." Ava had answered too quickly, too honestly. Z might think she was strange, reading a book for younger kids over and over. A strange scaredy-cat.

Z rose and plucked the same hardcover from her bookshelf. Ava was impressed. Z's room seemed pretty disorganized. "I love this book," Z said. She plopped onto the rug beside Ava and flipped the pages, looking at the drawings. "Ha. Templeton, the rat, is funny."

"Yeah." But Ava couldn't help jumping to the book's heartbreaking ending. Like Ava's mom, Charlotte didn't get to see her babies grow up. "It's a really sad book."

"I love sad books. Sometimes I choose one because it's sad."

"You do?" Ava couldn't imagine making herself sad on purpose. "Why?"

Z sat cross-legged, one knee jittering. "Doesn't it feel good to let it out?"

Ava straightened. Z seemed to be saying that feeling bad could help you feel good sometimes. Ava had never thought of that.

"Charlotte saves Wilbur." Z stretched her purple gum out of her mouth and swung it around her finger. "And he's friends with her daughters."

Ava nodded. That made the ending slightly easier. She'd just reread the part where Charlotte catches a fly in her web. Wilbur is horrified that she plans to suck its blood for breakfast. He's unsure about the spider. But those kinds of doubts and worries are normal, the book said, when you find a new friend.

Ava had forgotten that part.

———

That night, Ava couldn't help thinking about the secret sticks as she and Z brushed their teeth in The Girlfriend's bathroom. What if she hadn't put them back exactly where they belonged? What if The Girlfriend noticed?

Z caught Ava's eye in the mirror. "I have rabies," she announced. Z growled and shook her head, spittle flying. Foamy toothpaste dribbled onto her chin.

It was super gross. And hilarious. Also, Ava needed to report to her friends that unlike Emma's big sister, Z rinsed the sink.

"You can sleep with me," Z said as they returned to her room. "Up in my bed."

Ava appreciated the offer, but falling asleep was hard enough without worrying about actually falling. She eyed the recliner. If she slept there, the platform could fall and crush her. Still, it seemed safer than the alternative. "Could I sleep in the chair?"

"When my friends stay over, we all sleep up here." Z scrambled up the ladder. "There's plenty of room."

"Yeah." Ava took a breath. "I'm not the biggest fan of heights."

For a moment Ava worried Z would call her a scaredy-cat again. Without warning, she sailed from her bed and yelled for her mother to bring more sheets and a blanket.

Z was still yelling the next morning.

"I told you!" It sounded as if she were outside her bedroom—shouting at someone in Nebraska. "I looked there!" Pause. "No!"

As Ava snuggled into her recliner nest, it hit her. She wasn't an Ava pancake!

"I didn't," Z yelled. Then: "What?" And: "I can't hear you!" Until, finally, footsteps thumped downstairs.

Ava descended a little later. Rumpled sheets covered the sofa where Dad had slept. The TV news was on. Headlines rolled across the bottom of the screen: three rescuers injured searching for missing climber; bear rummages through eight unlocked vehicles in Estes Park; mountain lion creeps around Aurora backyard…Ava wanted to race back upstairs and hide under her blanket.

Meanwhile, Dad drank coffee at the island. The Girlfriend stood at the counter, her back to Ava, making sandwiches. Z stomped around in boots that laced up above her ankles, trying to juggle two oranges. They dropped immediately, two dull thumps on the wooden floor. She picked them up and marched over to Dad. "Show me again," Z demanded, and he got up, grabbed a third orange from the fruit bowl, and juggled. How many secrets was he keeping from her?

"Remember," Dad said, "your arc shouldn't be higher than eye level."

It took all Ava's willpower not to fly at him, shrieking like a vicious, plague-crazed Colorado ground squirrel.

She wanted to scream: Are you starting a new family with your long-distance girlfriend?

And: How could you rent a cabin in the mountains behind my back?

And: Why didn't you tell me you could juggle?

But Ava wasn't one to act rashly. She needed to talk to him privately.

"Ava's up," Z yelled as Ava sprinted to the bathroom. "When can we go?"

"Soon," The Girlfriend said. "Inside voice."

Clomp, clomp, clompclompclomp. "Guess what, Ava?" Z

shouted because, apparently, it was National Shouting Day. "You get to go to Red Rocks!"

"Come help me with the trail mix," The Girlfriend said.

Clomp, clomp, clomp.

Ava didn't know what Red Rocks was, but rocks usually were outdoors, and in Colorado, that meant danger. She had to force herself to leave the bathroom.

Dad, The Betrayer/Secret Juggler, sat again with his coffee. "Morning, Baby Ava Girl."

Z might have snickered. Ava wasn't sure.

Because: Ava's heart stopped. Her lungs stopped. Every cell in Ava's body stopped.

Cause of death: Extreme embarrassment by father.

How could he call her that in front of Z and The Girlfriend? Why had Ava never really noticed that the nickname started with "baby"?

"Did you sleep okay?" The Girlfriend asked. "We have a sleeping bag, if—"

"I like the chair." Ava wanted to peek at The Girlfriend's stomach.

"We're going to Red Rocks," Z said, crunching trail mix. "It's this outdoor concert place made out of huge, cool rocks." She grinned. "Guess what color they are?"

"Red?" Ava's voice came out unsure.

Z laughed. "Well, yeah."

"It's a natural amphitheater," The Girlfriend said. "All kinds of big stars perform there."

"Rodrigo shoots there all the time." Z raised a booted foot. "He gave me these."

"Don't talk with your mouth full," The Girlfriend said.

The doorbell rang, and Z thudded across the living room.

"Are we going to a concert?" Ava asked.

"No," Dad said, butting in. "We'll just look around."

That sounded strange. Ava couldn't imagine people visiting the Iowa State Fair main stage to see nothing.

Two boys stood at the door with skateboards.

"Sorry, guys," Z said instead of hello. "We're going to Red Rocks."

"Sick!" one said.

"Dude," the other guy agreed.

"Catch you later." Z returned to the kitchen. "You can run up the stairs too. At Red Rocks. It's a killer workout."

"Oh." That sounded dangerous. "Were those boys your friends?" Ava's stomach twisted. It's not like Z's enemies—if she had any—would want to hang out.

Z's brows wrinkled. "Aren't you friends with guys?"

"Yeah," Ava said. "We only see each other at school, though." With everything spread so far apart, it's not like Ava and her friends could pop over to each other's houses. Did Z go on dates, though? Was one of those guys her boyfriend? What if…

No. Z was way too young to have a baby. Plus: She wasn't that mature. Her stomach looked regular too.

If Z was having a baby, that meant she'd gotten her period, like Kylie and Emma. Ava hadn't. It meant Z had kissed a boy and more—much, much more. Kissing someone—in a lovey-dovey way, not like kissing Dad or Grandmom on the cheek—seemed awkward and terrifying. You'd have to aim carefully, and what if you accidentally had bad breath or coughed? What if you suddenly had to throw up and it happened so fast you did it in the other person's mouth? A trikillion things could go wrong. The only good thing about Z being pregnant would be that Dad had nothing to do with it.

Conversation Starters with Z:

- When you were in fifth grade, did the girls in your class watch the movie <u>Wonderful, Blossoming You?</u> Did you get free deodorant?
- Have you read <u>Are You There God? It's Me Margaret</u> by Judy Blume?
- Period panties: Pro or con?

CHAPTER 6

As The Girlfriend's Jeep hurtled west out of Denver, the landscape grew rugged, and Ava's uneasiness swelled. Somewhere out here: mountains.

"Z?" Ava whispered. "Red Rocks isn't…in the mountains, is it?"

Z looked up from her phone. "Nope."

It was the best news Ava had heard all morning. A few minutes later, though, her chest squeezed. Because: The Girlfriend drove straight toward mountains!

"Z!" Ava stabbed her finger out the window.

Z frowned, then laughed. "Mountains are big, Ava."

Her tone carried a hint of attitude, but how could she deny that those landforms were big? They weren't like little Iowa hills you could run up in a minute. They were huge, rolling humps covered with grass and trees. They looked like photos of mountains without snowy tops.

"They're foothills," The Girlfriend called back.

If Dad had given Ava more time to prepare for the trip, she would have learned about foothills. What if they were as dangerous as mountains?

As Z had promised, the actual Red Rocks were huge and cool. The rocks' stripes—pale pink, peach, blazing sunset orange, and, of course, red—showed how sediment had built up over time. The stripes were diagonal, though, as if a giant had set them down sideways. Ava appreciated all of this from the car. She didn't need to get out.

"Should we start at the amphitheater?" The Girlfriend asked.

It wasn't really a question. They were determined to walk around, and Ava had to join them.

The sun, hidden yesterday, now glowed against a robin's-egg sky. The group followed a wide ramp up and around colossal rock formations, then climbed several flights of stairs to the amphitheater. A sign said: "Altitude getting to you? Use our pulse rate monitor located outside the Visitor Center." Ava wasn't sure what good that would do someone suffering from altitude sickness, but at least it was a reminder about Colorado's defective air.

The amphitheater resembled a large rock bowl with a stage at one end, rows of seats rising from it, and massive rock formations around those. The seats were cut into the rock, inlaid with smooth wood, and curved, unbroken from one end of the theater to the other.

Ava was shocked at how many people ran along the rows, zigzagging to the top. Others did push-ups or stretches on the benches. There were lots of dogs, some jogging with their owners. A Mouse-shaped pain burned Ava's heart. When they returned to Z's, she needed to call Mrs. Mendez and check on them. She hadn't had a chance yesterday.

"Have you been to a show here?" Ava had to look way up, because tall Z had jumped onto the seats.

"Rodrigo was going to take me to Billie Eilish but it didn't work out. We had tickets to Logic, too, but…" Z glanced over at their parents. "*Someone* said, 'His lyrics are inappropriate.'" She spoke in an exaggerated, high-pitched scolding tone.

Ava laughed.

"Rodrigo and I were mad," Z continued in her normal voice. "He's my parent too."

Ava nodded. She'd never been to a concert that wasn't in a school gym. It would have been super amazing to attend one at Red Rocks, especially at night, under the stars.

Z jumped, landing uncomfortably close to Ava. "Let's race!"

Before Ava knew what was happening, Z shot up the stairs. The odds of Ava chasing her: 0 percent. She wandered over to Dad and The Girlfriend.

"I'm sorry for Z's bad manners," The Girlfriend said. She pointed past the highest row. "There's a museum at the top. Do you want to go up there?"

They'd already climbed so much, and it looked very, very far. Z was making good progress, though.

They took it slow, but all three were breathing hard when they reached the top. A large patio outside the Visitors Center over-looked the amphitheater and rolling foothills—not mountains. Scores of people milled about, admiring the views and taking pictures. Ava heard Spanish, English in a British accent, and what might have been Arabic and Japanese.

"Hey, slowpokes," Z said, dancing around them.

As they entered the building, Z ran ahead again. Apparently, she never worried about getting lost—or kidnapped. Ava viewed the exhibits on her own, with Dad safely in sight.

One display in particular drew her interest. A sign titled "Health at High Altitude" said the air at Red Rocks, at 6,250 feet, offered only 80 percent of the oxygen that was available at sea level, where it was easiest to breathe. The top of Vail's ski lift, at ten thousand feet, had only 66 percent of the oxygen compared to sea level. The display also included sections called "The Sun—Intensified," warning about harmful UV rays, stronger at high altitude; and "Rattlesnake Territory," about Red Rocks offering a prime habitat for the poisonous snakes.

Ava fetched Dad from the geology section. "Come see this," she said, tugging his arm. Maybe "Health at High Altitude" would convince him to cancel their cabin reservation?

Dad studied the sign. "Interesting."

"Did you read all of it? High altitude is dangerous."

"You haven't been drinking, have you?" The display said to avoid alcohol in the first forty-eight hours.

"Dad." This wasn't the time to joke. Plus: How could he act like everything was fine when he was keeping this enormous mountain secret from her, like a lie?

They wandered to the next display, about the early days of the park. With The Girlfriend still at the geology section, this was

Ava's chance to figure out if she and Dad were serious enough to have a baby. Ava needed to act cool and casual, though. She didn't know what he knew. She didn't even know what *she* knew.

"Dad? I was thinking…" Dad's patience was one of his best qualities. He gave Ava space for her thoughts to become words. "Remember when I asked if…if you"—Ava swallowed—"if things are serious with you and Jenn?"

"Yeah?"

"Well…you kind of didn't answer."

Dad stiffened. "I didn't?" His voice sounded higher than usual.

"Not really."

"I want you to get to know Jenn and Z." He glanced at The Girlfriend and back to Ava. "You like them, don't you?"

"Yeah, but, Dad?" Ava's fingers found her watch. "You kind of didn't tell me…"

"If it's serious?"

"Yes!" Somehow, they'd fallen into some super-slow-motion alternative reality, each second excruciatingly embarrassing and lasting days.

"You know I love you more than anything, right? You're my number one, Baby Ava Girl."

Ava doubted this still was true but nodded.

"I care for Jenn very much, and I really want this to work, okay?" His eyes held Ava's, and almost against her will, she nodded. But what did "want this to work" mean exactly? Have a good vacation—or something more?

"What if you wanted to…"

After a long moment, Dad said, "Wanted to what?"

"I don't know." The Girlfriend was at "Health at High Altitude." Was she going slowly to let them talk? Maybe she was stuck in her own alternate reality. Ava took a breath. "What if you guys wanted to have a baby or something?"

Dad laughed, showing his white teeth. "We haven't gotten to the marriage part yet, Ava. We're a long way from babies."

Ava's insides melted with relief. Dad cleaned his glasses on his shirt and glanced again at The Girlfriend. "Anything else on your mind?"

Ava gripped her watch. Should she tell him about the sticks she'd found? "I…" Ava had to catch her breath. "You…"

Dad returned his glasses to his face and squinted, as if trying to read Ava's mind.

Ava tried again. "It's just…" What if The Girlfriend had cheated on him? That might break his heart. "I really didn't want to come to Colorado."

"I think you've mentioned that." Dad didn't sound annoyed. That was another nice thing about him. He was slow to anger. Ava didn't know much (anything) about boyfriends, but she figured Dad would be a good one. Why, then, was The Girlfriend having a baby with someone else? Why wasn't that guy here?

Maybe the sticks really were Z's?

Three-fourths of them wanted to hike, so Ava had to. She'd heard of hiking but wasn't clear on the particulars. As it turned out, it was walking—but in nature and hard.

The trail started with steep red-rock steps. Everyone knew walking uphill could be difficult, but Ava was surprised by how challenging it was to keep her footing while heading down. They descended single file. Ava grabbed the back of Dad's backpack to steady herself.

Meanwhile, Z—a nimble mountain goat in her Rodrigo hiking boots—bounded ahead.

After the stairs, the trail leveled out. It was the color of dry, red clay, with tiny white rocks, and it was narrow—they walked single file when they met a group coming from the other direction. The trail carved through a meadow dotted with yellow wildflowers and flanked by huge red and orange rocks.

"Isn't it beautiful, Ava?" Dad said.

"Shh," Ava said. "We need to listen for rattles."

"Ava." Dad suddenly sounded tired. "That sign said rattlesnakes aren't aggressive—"

"Unless they're surprised," Ava said. "Or cornered."

"Look at all the people." He raised his arms without dropping The Girlfriend's hand. "It's noisy," Dad continued. "If rattlesnakes are out here, they're hiding."

Ava had no doubt rattlesnakes were here. Besides this being a perfect habitat, the display said the most frequent wildlife encounters in Colorado were with rattlesnakes. (This was a surprise, considering the endless online library of Colorado charging elk videos.)

"They're scared of you, Ava," The Girlfriend said.

Ava plodded forward, listening for rattles, scanning for ground squirrels. Z, far in the distance, stopped, turned, and jogged back, practically floating on those long legs. Her deep purple hair gleamed in the sun.

She fell into step beside Ava. "Well?" Z quirked a single eyebrow.

"It's cool. Like another planet, almost."

Z looked at Ava. "You never said what you want to do. When you're older."

"Oh." Ava tried to think of a job as dangerous as astronaut. "Lion tamer." She gently bit her tongue to keep her face serious. "And flying trapeze artist." Ava's solemn face held for only a moment longer. "Who juggles fire."

"Yowza! I thought you were serious!" Z jumped to emphasize each sentence.

Ava did a tiny, pleased shrug.

"I totally believed you!" Z pointed at her. "You should be an actor. Or a spy! You could wear disguises and travel all over the world." She raised her sunglasses and squinted at Ava. "You're so small, you could squeeze into gnarly hiding places and eavesdrop on criminals."

Ava wasn't that small. Plus: She still had a lot of growing to do. Double plus: She didn't want anything to do with criminals. But Z's reaction gave her confidence to tiptoe into an important topic.

CHAPTER 7

The temperature had warmed as they hiked, but that wasn't the reason Ava's cheeks grew hot. "Uh...Z?" she said. "You know those boys who came over this morning? Is one of them your boyfriend or something?"

Z stopped and grabbed Ava's arm. "Tell me you're not one of those boy-crazy girls, Ava. You're not, are you?"

"No!"

Z looked skeptical. "I can't even with them." She released Ava's arm. "Those guys are friends. I told you."

"I know. Okay. I'm sorry."

Their feet, the wind, and distant voices of other hikers were the only sounds. Their parents lagged farther behind.

Ava cleared her throat. "One of my friends, Emma? Her big sister gets within two feet of a guy and starts flipping her hair and giggling."

"The hair flip," Z said with an exaggerated toss of her ponytail. "Classic."

"Giggling for no reason, Z. She laughs even if nothing's funny."

Z laughed.

"No one else is laughing," Ava said, cracking up too.

"Because nothing is funny," Z said, laughing harder.

"Yes!"

Z sobered. "You know how I said there's changes at middle school? Well, my friends…" Z stretched her arms overhead and let them drop. "That was a biggie. Getting a boyfriend was all they cared about. They talked for hours about some guy saying hey in the halls. What did it mean, you know?"

"Maybe it meant, 'hey,'" Ava said, shrugging.

"Right? When we hung out, they only wanted to watch makeup videos." Z exhaled. "It's like middle school ate their brains."

"I'm sorry."

"It's okay."

It wasn't, though. Z's friends had lost their brains, but Z had lost them. Ava couldn't imagine how hurt she'd feel if Kylie and Emma suddenly changed like that. It helped explain why Z had reacted so strongly to Ava's question about the guy friends. It also seemed even less likely that Z was pregnant.

"You know what else?" Z said. "All these girls—people I didn't even know—suddenly wanted to be my friends."

"You didn't want new friends?"

"Of course I did," Z snapped. "Just not like that."

"I don't—" Ava began.

"Because of Rodrigo. They wanted to meet him, I guess." Z shrugged her one-shoulder-higher shrug. "Or be on TV or something."

"They were using you? That's terrible."

"It's stupid. I can't make them famous." Z looked at her. "He's always been successful. But that show..." She sighed. "He's so busy, and it's like everyone knows him now."

The trail curved around red rock formations that looked like abstract sculptures.

"I'm sorry."

"It's fine." Z brightened. "I can't wait to see him!"

"He lives in Colorado, though, right?" Ava's plan—when she finally got one—would keep them in Denver. But Z could see her dad later.

"Yeah. But assignments come up, and the show shoots in LA."

"But if for some reason you don't see him Monday, you can still see him another time, right?" If Ava wasn't careful, she'd give away her plan before she had it.

"I guess I could see him Tuesday or the other days. And we're doing the Mud Run." Before Ava had a chance to ask what that was, Z continued, "I mean, we're there ten days. But I want to see him as much as possible."

Wait—

"I miss him. He gets me so much better than my mom."

Ten days?

In the mountains?

That couldn't be right.

Dad planned to spend ten of their fourteen Colorado days in the mountains—and hadn't told her? It was unthinkable. Impossible.

"Are you—" Ava stopped to catch her breath. "Do you mean—"

It couldn't be true.

"You're saying...ten days..." Ava's ears rang. "In the..."

Z glanced at their parents and then back to Ava. "He didn't tell you that, either?"

"You said Monday." Ava's chest tightened. "I thought..."

Z laughed. "Why would anyone go on a one-day vacation?"

Ava exhaled through her mouth. Her heart raced. Her fingertips tingled. She was dizzy.

"What's wrong?" Z's voice sounded far away.

Ava couldn't catch her breath.

This was her worst fear.

Especially in Colorado.

It was happening again.

"Ava." Mrs. Roberts's voice was sharp in her head. "Calm down!"

Ava and the school nurse didn't get along. Mrs. Roberts said Ava came to the office for every little thing. Actually, Ava did everything she could—enduring stomachaches, headaches, and other aches—to stay in class. Visiting the mean nurse was a last resort.

Mrs. Roberts was right in Ava's face, with her coffee breath and curly rainbow wig for Field Day. "You're okay," she said grimly. "Breathe."

As if Ava didn't want to.

As if Ava were being difficult.

As if she didn't understand that breathing was a big part of not dying.

"Eric," Z shouted. "Something's wrong with Ava!"

In a flash Dad was there, guiding Ava to the side of the trail, allowing two groups to pass. "What's happening?" He crouched. "Look at me, Baby Ava Girl."

The sun was too bright. Too hot. Sweat trickled down Ava's sides. Her insides burned. Her heart raced too fast, too fast. Her lungs weren't working.

"Ava." Dad's voice was low and urgent. "Are you thinking about rattlesnakes?"

Ava shook her head. Her tongue was a thick, fuzzy sock, too big for her mouth.

"Let's focus on breathing, okay?" Dad said. "No, wait. Sit first."

After a slight hesitation, Ava dropped to the rough ground.

"Good. Okay." Dad rubbed his hands, bubbling with new energy. "Everything's okay."

The tiny white rocks poked Ava's skin like sixtillion-fobillion needles.

"Nice and slow." Dad rubbed her back. "Fill your belly like a big, fat balloon."

But Ava's lungs had shrunk. Plus: There was 20 percent less oxygen here than at sea level.

After a while—two minutes, two hours, Ava had no clue—the slow, deep breathing loosened her clenched muscles, cooled the inside fire, and expanded her too-small lungs. Her heart still galloped but had slowed enough so that it didn't feel like it would pop.

Ava blinked at the meadow. The impressive red rocks. The trail.

"Feeling better?" Dad passed her a water bottle. "When you're ready, we'll meet Jenn and Z at the Trading Post. No hurry."

Ava stood, her legs as shaky as a newborn calf's, and brushed off her shorts and legs.

"Lean on me. You're sure you're okay?"

Ava nodded.

They followed the red clay trail, retracing their path. "Do you think maybe you were too focused on rattlesnakes?" Dad asked.

Ava prickled with irritation. Was he blaming her? She pressed her lips together, fighting the words straining to come out. It was too soon. She didn't have a plan.

"It's good to be careful," Dad was saying. "But you take it too far sometimes, Ava."

"Dr. C. said it can happen out of the blue," Ava said. "There doesn't have to be a reason."

Dr. C. also had said stress and nervousness might trigger it. If anyone was to blame, it was Dad. Ava had just learned about his secret, ten-day mountain plan—ten days!—when she'd started feeling sick.

A fiery energy whirled in her chest. After only two days in Colorado, Ava had become an expert at identifying at least one emotion: anger.

They'd reached the steep rock steps. "Are you okay to go up?" Dad asked.

"Yeah." Ava clutched his backpack as they began their slow trek. "Dad?"

He stopped and turned, worry creasing his forehead. "Are you feeling faint?"

Ava couldn't wait. "Z said we're going to the mountains. For ten days."

Dad frowned and rubbed the back of his neck.

Ava searched his face. "That's not true, right?"

When he finally met her eyes, Ava realized with a jolt that Z had been right. Her knees wobbled, and Dad grabbed her arm.

"Jenn told me about this awesome place," he said.

He talked some more, but Ava couldn't hear.

He loved The Girlfriend more than her. And The Girlfriend was (probably) pregnant and (probably) a cheater. The realization blasted Ava's heart like a bomb.

When they reached the top of the stairs, Dad smiled and waved at Z and The Girlfriend, who hurried toward them from the Red Rocks gift shop.

"People from all over the world come to Colorado to see the mountains," Dad said, as if he were a tour guide. "And they stay at this place Jenn knows. You'll love it, Baby Ava Girl, and then you're going to be embarrassed you made such a fuss."

A fuss? That's what he thought her concerns were, some kind of silly *fuss*?

"Hey," Z called, jogging to them, her mom close behind. "Are you okay?"

"Are you feeling better?" The Girlfriend asked.

"Yeah," Ava said before spinning to face Dad. "Colorado has more lightning deaths—most of them in the mountains—than almost any other state."

"Did you have a seizure?" Z asked.

"Charging moose! Hungry mountain lions!" Ava's quaking voice grew louder despite the embarrassment of people overhearing. "Ground squirrels with plague!"

"Ava," Dad said, "calm down."

"Wildfires! Rocks fall on people, Dad." Ava spread her arms. "Rocks as big as cars. People fall off mountains. They're—"

Z looked around. "Who fell?"

"They're out for a hike," Ava continued, "like us today—and—ahhhh!"

"Ava. Stop."

"Oh, no! I fell off the mountain! Thanks for the great vacation where I died, Dad."

"Stop it." It was his firmest, no-nonsense tone.

But Ava couldn't. Wouldn't. She lowered her voice. "I guess you and your girlfriend would be happy if I was out of the picture," she said.

"Shut up!" Dad rushed toward her.

Ava shuffled back.

"Shut! Up! Right now!"

"Eric!" The Girlfriend moved toward them and put a hand on his arm.

Dad and Ava never said "shut up." It was a rule.

"Ava," Dad whispered. "I'm sorry." He hunched over, hands on his knees, breathless.

"What's happening?" Z asked.

It was embarrassing that Z and The Girlfriend were listening to Ava and Dad's personal, private business. But this was important. "When did she tell you about this place?"

Dad straightened and turned. "Don't ever say that again." His face looked sunburned.

"I can't even—"

Dad waved aside her question. "You said I'd be happier if you were gone. That was"—he shut his eyes for a moment—"very hurtful, Ava."

Ava looked at her tennis shoes. "I'm sorry."

"I mean it, Ava Louise. If I lost you—"

Ava looked up at him. "Why didn't you tell me?"

"Oh." Z turned to her mom. "She didn't know we were going to the mountains."

"Let's give them some space," The Girlfriend said, leading Z away.

"I'd never let anything hurt you, Ava. You know that." Dad ran a hand over his mouth. "We'll finish this…later."

Ava's heart pounded. Why hadn't he told her? Plus: He hadn't answered her question about when The Girlfriend had told him about the place. Double plus: Why did he get to decide their talk was over?

CHAPTER 8

The Girlfriend had brought PB&Js for a picnic, but they decided to eat at home.

"Are you sick?" Z asked as they buckled up in the Jeep's backseat. "What happened?"

Ava shook her head. What could she say? She didn't understand it herself. What Ava did know: If she told Z about the sudden fire inside her, the dizziness and tingling, the cramping, and how she couldn't breathe, she'd have to tell her about Field Day. Then Z would think Ava was weird or crazy—or both.

"You can't come to Colorado and not go to the mountains," Z said, as if it were the law. "You want to meet Rodrigo, don't you?"

"Of course." That was true, but why did they have to meet in the mountains?

Plus: At the moment, Ava was sick of fathers.

Back at the town house, The Girlfriend insisted that Ava rest in her bed. "Is that comfortable?" she asked, smooshing a pillow behind Ava's head. "I think we did too much too soon. I'm so sorry, Ava." She turned to Dad. "Did you see that altitude display? It's no joke."

"Mm-hmm," Dad said, as if he didn't want to take sides against dangerous altitude.

"Feel better, sweet pickle," The Girlfriend said, easing the door closed.

The way she said it, her voice so tender and full of affection, and the way she'd squished Ava's pillows just so, Ava couldn't imagine The Girlfriend being a cheater. If she was having a baby with somebody else, that guy—not Dad—would have been here.

What if she wasn't even pregnant, though? What if those sticks were from her pregnancy with Z? Ava wasn't sure why The Girlfriend would have kept them, but maybe she'd forgotten about them? They *had* been way at the back of the closet. Ava's chest loosened.

"She's pretty great, huh?" Dad said, pulling a cushy reading chair closer to the bed.

Ava stiffened. No one had called her "sweet pickle" before, and it was both nice and funny because Dad was allergic to pickles but her mom had loved them. But she wasn't going to praise Dad for picking an awesome girlfriend. Living in Colorado was a deal-breaker.

She felt his stare as she stroked her watch. "When were you going to tell me?"

"Tomorrow."

"One day?"

Dad set his glasses on the nightstand and rubbed his eyes.

"Obviously, we're still figuring out transitions. We'll talk to Dr. C. about it."

"The mountains aren't safe."

"Ava." Dad raised his hands in a "stop" motion. "You've told me how you feel."

"This isn't about feelings. Those are facts, Dad. Facts!"

Dad pulled his phone from his shorts pocket and tapped the screen. "Here's a fact. Nearly eighty-seven million people visited Colorado last year. I can use the internet, too, Ava."

A bunch of people came to Colorado. Big deal. It didn't take away the hazards.

"You're a bright girl," he said, "but you're still a child. You don't know everything."

She knew his girlfriend might be pregnant. Or her daughter. But probably not.

Dad sighed, his face and shoulders drooping as if he were a balloon that had lost its air. "I've heard your concerns, Ava. I really have." He held her gaze, making sure she understood. "I promise we'll be careful. I'm not going to discuss it anymore."

This was his idea of finishing their talk?

"I know your anxiety is hard, Baby Ava Girl, and you can't help it." He eyed her fingers on her watch. "You're learning to deal with it, and that's wonderful. I'm proud of you."

There was no point in talking more. Dad's mind was made up. But so was Ava's. She needed to find a way to keep them in Denver. "Can I borrow your phone?" she asked. "I forgot to call Mrs. Mendez yesterday."

He handed it to her, walked to the door, and paused. "I know you're mad, but you need to trust me. It's my job to keep you safe."

Dad would do anything to protect Ava—jump in front of a runaway train, take a bullet, wrestle a plague-crazed ground squirrel. For sure. But Ava had grown up with a hard lesson: No matter how much Dad loved her, he couldn't stop bad things from happening. Avoiding dangerous places like the mountains—all of Colorado, really—was a no-brainer.

As soon as he left, Ava noticed his glasses on The Girlfriend's nightstand. At home he always was taking them off to read or work on his laptop and then losing them. He didn't need them to see up close, but he couldn't watch TV or drive without them.

Ava picked them up, careful not to smudge the glass, and tucked them under the chair's seat cushion. Without his glasses, Dad couldn't wander around the mountains. Safely, at least.

But he could get new ones. Ava needed a better plan.

Ava was talking to Mrs. Mendez when Dad returned to The Girlfriend's bedroom. "I need to go," Ava whispered.

"Enjoy your new friend," Mrs. Mendez said, "and then come home and tell me about all your wonderful adventures. Don't worry about perrito."

Ava smiled. *Perrito* meant "little dog" in Spanish—and Mouse weighed one hundred pounds. "I miss him so much. All of you." A potato-sized lump lodged in her throat. "Good luck with bowling! Te quiero, Mrs. Mendez."

"I love you too, my sweet girl."

Ava handed Dad the phone. Then he settled—as if in slow motion—back into the chair. On top of the cushion on top of his glasses.

"How's everybody doing?" Dad asked.

"Good." Could he feel them?

"Hey." Dad looked around. "Have you seen my glasses?"

"What?" Ava's voice squeaked.

"I lost my glasses again."

"Oh, uh…nope. Haven't seen them. Sorry."

"I'm sure they'll turn up. If you're feeling better, why don't you find Z?"

When he left, Ava slipped off the bed, lifted a corner of the cushion, and exhaled.

It was a miracle. Dad's glasses were fine.

She picked them up—but, surprisingly, held only half. It took her a moment to realize the nose bridge had cracked cleanly down the middle. The frame was broken in two.

A headache bloomed above Ava's left eyebrow. She'd only wanted to hide them. On top of that, she'd looked Dad in the eye and lied. She wanted to run and confess. He'd hold her for a long time and whisper, "It's okay, Baby Ava Girl." She wanted them to be the way they were. Before The Girlfriend. Before Denver. Before the mountains.

Ava tucked Dad's glasses under the bed. Maybe it would look like they'd fallen there.

CHAPTER 9

Even though Ava still was furious with Dad, she hated seeing him squint at the baseball game the next afternoon.

"Go Rockies!" Z shouted and turned to Ava. "Did you see that play?"

Z, The Girlfriend, and Dad were into the game, especially The Girlfriend, who felt the umpires needed glasses as much as Dad.

Ava had a bigger worry. She needed a plan to keep them in Denver tomorrow. "Hey," she said, nudging Z, "could you tell your mom to ask my dad to let me borrow his phone?"

When the message reached Dad, he leaned forward and stared down the row at Ava. She smiled and waved—slightly more exaggerated than usual to make sure he saw her. When his phone made its way to her, Ava opened the internet and typed: "how to stop someone from going somewhere."

Someone had asked that exact question in a forum. Most of the answers were unhelpful. Chain him to the wall. Unless you're their parent, you can't do anything. Besides illegal things, nothing. Only one answer offered hope: Hide their keys. The Girlfriend kept her purse on a wall hook by the back door. But if Ava got caught looking for her keys, The Girlfriend might think she was trying to steal her money or something. Also, she might have a spare set of keys.

On the second page of her search results, Ava found "Put a Stop to Your Anxiety with These 8 Simple Steps." What did that have to do with keeping someone from going somewhere? She tried several more searches, including "how to stop something from happening" and "how to stop someone from taking a trip." That turned up "How Not to Let Anxiety Stop You from Traveling." She hated getting results that didn't match her question.

Z, The Girlfriend, and Dad were on their feet. Ava stood, and Z gave her a high five.

Maybe Ava could learn how to let the air out of tires? But that would be another temporary roadblock. She returned to her seat and the internet.

To her surprise, a mechanic had posted a four-minute video showing how to temporarily disable a car. You might want to do this to test your car's starter or battery, he said. All you had to do was locate the fuel pump fuse, which looked like a Lego, and pull it out. When you start the car, the mechanic said, "it'll crank, but it won't fire." To demonstrate, he turned the key in the car ignition. The car shuddered, whined, and died. It was awesome.

The only problem: His car wasn't a Jeep, and he'd used his owner's manual to find the fuse location. Where would The Girlfriend keep her owner's manual? What possible reason could Ava give for wanting to read it?

More searching quickly revealed that some Jeeps were different—different better. You didn't need the owner's manual. A diagram showing the car's fuses was printed under the hood. You looked at the diagram's labeled boxes and matched them right there with the real thing.

Ava would have to do it that night, after everyone went to bed. That meant sneaking past Dad sleeping on the sofa.

Z, her voice hoarse from cheering the Rockies to victory, talked more than ever after lights-out. When Z's snores began and Ava finally descended the stairs, she heard faint music and a strange sound. Peeking into the main room, her eyes strained through the shadows. The dim light wasn't from a night-light, as she'd expected. Instead, the flickering glow came from candles, which was alarming, since burning candles should never be left alone…

Dad.

The Girlfriend.

Lip-locked.

Ava dropped to the floor, her nightgown pooling around her. Wet kissing sounds came from the sofa. Ava wanted to stab her eardrums and eyeballs and dash back to the recliner. But this was her only chance to take the fuel pump fuse. Slowly, slowly, Ava crawled to the armchair. She let her heart settle, and then, very slowly, very quietly, snuck toward the kitchen island.

"Ava?" Dad sounded more puzzled than angry. "What are you doing?"

Ava halted, like a bunny who thinks freezing makes her invisible. She looked up at his gross kiss face. "I—uh…"

The Girlfriend joined Dad, smoothing her hair. "Hi, Ava."

They didn't even look embarrassed. Ava jumped up, quivering from the epic weirdness. "I need a drink," she said. "And I left something in your car."

"Oh," The Girlfriend said. "I can get it—"

"That's okay. You're…busy." Ava's face burst into flames.

"The garage door is locked." The Girlfriend headed toward her purse. "Use this one." She held up the smallest key on a Colorado Rockies keychain. "I don't think the car is locked, but if it is, push this button. The garage has an overhead light by the door. Are you sure—"

"It's fine."

"You're supposed to be sleeping," Dad said, as if only realizing this.

"After this, I'll go right to bed."

Ava headed toward the back door. But trying to walk normally, as if she had not been discovered skulking on the floor in the dark while Dad made out with his girlfriend, as if she were a nice person and not someone preparing to carry out a major car-disabling plan, threw off Ava's stride. Her legs couldn't remember what to do.

Two porch lights illuminated the back patio, and Ava easily unlocked the garage door and found the light. She could do this. She could. The Jeep's hood release was on the inside door, below the steering wheel and control panel, exactly where the internet said it would be. That raised the hood slightly, but she still needed to release the safety latch.

Ava reached under the hood, her fingers exploring strange metal shapes. Her hand couldn't fit in the space, and it was awkward. Nothing felt like a latch. She peered into the dark, narrow gap but couldn't see anything.

How long before Dad checked on her? Ava thought through each step again. She pushed and pulled. She even tugged the hood from the top.

It didn't budge.

Ava whispered a very bad swear and "stupid car." She kicked the tire—hard.

"Ow! Ow! Ow!" Ava collapsed on the dirty floor and cradled her bare foot. Pain streaked through her red toes. Her knuckles bled slightly from where they'd scraped under the hood. Ava stood, dusted off, and hobbled to the door.

When she entered the town house, Dad was waiting. "I'll take the keys," he said.

If Ava had been thinking straight, she'd have said she'd lost them. He would have said, "How is it possible to lose the keys walking from the garage?" But there wouldn't have been anything he could have done except look for them. Without his glasses.

But Ava wasn't thinking—straight or otherwise—and she hadn't expected him to pounce on her, practically. When he held out his hand, she set the keys in it.

"You didn't find it?"

"Oh. No." Ava had forgotten her lie. "I'd better get to bed."

Toes throbbing, Ava tried not to limp as she passed through the dining room, the kitchen, the living room. Dad's eyes were twin x-ray lasers burning into her back, exposing her lies.

Nothing on the internet had indicated opening the hood would be a problem. She couldn't worry about that now. It was time for Plan B.

Box Breathing

1. Inhale through your nose while counting to 4.
2. Hold your breath while counting to 4.
3. Exhale through your mouth with a "whoosh" while counting to 4.
4. Hold your breath while counting to 4.
5. Repeat.

CHAPTER 10

"Wake up, sleepyheads," The Girlfriend whispered.

The room was dark. Ava curled her toes. They still hurt.

The Girlfriend parted the hanging curtain. "Good morning."

Ava moaned and held her stomach.

"Are you okay?" The Girlfriend peered closer.

"Look out," Z yelled. She flew from the bed, stumbled, collapsed, and rolled onto her rear. "Whoa," she said, laughing.

"Mackenzie. Use the ladder."

"When can we leave?" Z said, popping up. "Can we go now?"

"Don't you think you should put on some clothes first?" The Girlfriend teased. She turned back to Ava. "Are you okay?"

"I don't feel good." Ava made her voice tiny.

"Dressed," Z announced, pulling a T-shirt over her head as she strode into the hideout. She studied Ava. "You're sick?"

Ava hoped Z was right, that she was a good actor. "I don't know." Downplaying it seemed more believable. "Maybe?"

"You can't be sick," Z said.

"I'll get Eric," The Girlfriend said.

As soon as her mom left, Z sprang on Ava. "Are you faking?"

"No!" Ava worked to keep her face innocent. "Move back. I don't want you to get this."

"It seems strange," Z said, pacing in front of the recliner like a lawyer before a jury, "that you'd be sick the day we're going to the mountains."

"Yeah," Ava said. "I'm fine, probably." She winced as she shifted positions. "If I was faking, don't you think I'd have started last night at least?"

In fact, she would have—if she hadn't counted on the Jeep-disabling plan.

"Besides," Ava continued. "I can't be fake sick for ten days." This was a terrifying truth. She needed another plan—fast.

"You don't look so great," Z said. "Is it your stomach?"

The adults proved even easier to fool, and Ava was pleased to return to The Girlfriend's comfy bed. But she couldn't relax, of course. She needed a new plan—one that would keep them in Denver until Ava and Dad flew home.

"We should call the lodge." The Girlfriend's voice carried from the hallway. "Let them know we won't be there today."

"Good idea," Dad said.

Later, when he stopped by, Ava could barely look at him. This was all his fault. Plus: She couldn't stop thinking about those cringey kiss sounds.

"How are you feeling?" Dad asked, sitting on the edge of the bed.

"Sick," she said, sounding like her regular, healthy self.

"We'll go when you're feeling better."

I'LL NEVER FEEL BETTER, Ava's glare said.

I ORDER YOU TO FEEL BETTER, Dad's glare answered.

THE MOUNTAINS ARE TREACHEROUS, Ava's glare countered.

I DON'T CARE BECAUSE I LOVE MY GIRLFRIEND MORE THAN YOU, Dad's glare said.

"Can I use your phone? I forgot to ask Mrs. Mendez something yesterday."

That was another lie. But Mrs. Mendez's youngest grandson, Arturo, liked messing with cars. Maybe he could help Ava get the Jeep's stupid hood open.

"Not too long," Dad said, handing it to her. "You need rest."

After he left, Ava clicked on the list of phone numbers from the most recent calls. Mrs. Mendez's number was second. The most recent call didn't have an Iowa area code. Ava's insides spun. She pressed the strange number. The phone rang once, twice, three times.

"It's a great day to play at Soaring Eagle Resort," a woman said. "How may I help you?"

Something tickled Ava's brain.

"Hello? Is someone there?"

The Girlfriend had asked Dad to call the lodge, to say they wouldn't be there today.

"Hello?" the woman repeated.

Was Soaring Eagle Resort a lodge? A lodge in the mountains?

"H—hello?" Ava said. "Hello?"

The Soaring Eagle woman had hung up.

Ava shut her eyes for a moment. She set the phone on her lap, exhaled, and shook out her hands. Then she picked it up and pressed the number.

"It's a great day to play at Soaring Eagle Resort. How may I help you?"

Ava swallowed.

"Hello?"

"Uh." Ava had to catch her breath. "Hello?"

"Yes. How may I help you?"

"We called this morning." Ava imitated Mrs. Roberts's stern tone to sound grown-up. "About…our reservations."

"I'm sorry," the woman. "It's noisy. I couldn't hear you."

Ava repeated herself, her heart a bucking bronco.

"What's the name of your party?"

"Headly. Eric Headly from Iowa." Ava rubbed her thigh with her free hand.

"Let's see, you're scheduled to arrive today for ten days in our Eagle's Nest cabin. Oh, there's a note…"

Ava bit her lip.

"You can't come today," the woman said, "but we're expecting you tomorrow?"

"We can't come. At all."

"Did you say you won't be staying at all?"

"That's correct." Ava was proud of her mature vocabulary.

"That's a shame," the woman said. "Could I speak to Mr. Headly, please?"

"He told me to call." Fire scorched Ava's neck. "He's...in the bathroom."

"Unfortunately, we're unable to issue a refund on last-minute cancellations. Could he call when he's free?"

"He's sick. It's..." Ava shut her eyes. "Coming out both ends."

"Oh. Well, how about this?" The Soaring Eagle woman suddenly sounded excited. "Why don't you keep the reservation? That way, if he feels better, and you're able to get here, even for a day, the cabin would be available. You've already paid. It's one of our most beautiful cabins."

"Uh—"

"This is one of our busiest times," the woman continued, because this conversation would never end. "We're booked, the whole county is this time of year."

Ava could stop this. Dad, The Girlfriend, and Z would never know what she'd tried to do. Ava could say okay, and the reservation would remain, no harm done. But Colorado's mountains were dangerous! She couldn't forget that—or what she'd witnessed the night before in the candlelit living room.

"He's...very contagious."

"Oh, my. I'm sorry."

Z entered The Girlfriend's bedroom. "Are you feeling better?" she asked, sinking into the chair next to the bed.

Ava motioned to the phone.

Z's voice dropped to a loud whisper. "Are you feeling better?" She leaned back, stretched her purple gum far out of her mouth, and whipped it around her finger.

Ava mimed—again—that she couldn't talk. Z's eyeballs drilled into her. Ava didn't have a choice. She had to do this.

"Hello? Miss? Are you there?"

"Yeah. Sorry." Ava glanced at Z. She'd been so excited to see her dad.

"Are we keeping the reservation then?"

"No." Ava stared at her lap and certainly, definitely, not at Z. "We can't."

"Life throws curveballs, doesn't it? I'm sorry. I'll need your confirmation code when you're ready."

"My what?"

"It's a four-digit number. Mr. Headly would have received it in an email."

Ava opened Dad's emails and scrolled. "I—I think I found it. Two, eight, zero, five?"

"That's right," the woman said. "And the last four digits of the credit card on file? It should be in the same email."

"Oh." Ava swallowed. "Yeah. Three, three, five, eight."

"All right. We'll email a cancellation confirmation. I hope Mr. Headly feels better soon, and that we can serve you in the future."

"Thanks." Ava set the phone down beside her, pressed her palms into her eyes, and breathed. What had she done?

"Who was that?" Z snapped her gum. "Are you feeling better?"

Ava looked up. Maybe Z really did care about her.

"I really want to see Rodrigo." Z stood. "Lunch is ready, if you feel good enough."

"I'll be there in a sec," Ava said.

An email from the resort pinged Dad's inbox. Ava deleted it.

When she arrived at the table, Dad was at the counter, his back turned. "The soup's for you," Z said, her mouth already full of sandwich, a blob of purple gum stuck to her plate.

Ava stared into the steamy bowl of chicken noodle. After canceling their reservations, her stomachache was real. She looked up and gasped.

"Found my glasses," Dad said.

They sat on his face at a slight angle, a wad of white medical tape circling the center. It was Classic Halloween Nerd Costume. Except it was June. And not a costume.

Z laughed. "That looks weird."

"Yep," Dad agreed. He poured them all lemonade. "I'm glad to see you eating, Ava. Are you feeling better?"

"Where'd you find them?" Ava asked.

A line appeared between Dad's eyebrows, and Ava's guts splashed on the floor. The only way her guilt would have been more obvious was if a sign with flashing lights had appeared over her head announcing: AVA DID IT.

"Jenn's room," Dad said, sitting. "They got stepped on or something."

"You're feeling better, right?" Z said, leaning toward Ava.

Ava looked at Dad, bracing for the guilty verdict. "You do look like you're feeling a little better," he said.

The Girlfriend stared too. All those eyes. Ava picked a salt crystal off a pale cracker.

"We can still go today," Z said, bouncing in her seat, "if you're better."

"We should probably wait," The Girlfriend said, "to be safe."

"She could rest in the car. Couldn't you, Ava?" Z said. "I could text Rodrigo and tell him I'll be there today after all."

Ava turned to Dad. "Aren't you going to get your glasses fixed?"

If he hadn't known she was guilty before, he did now. She sounded like a guilty person in a movie or TV show.

Dad shook his head. "My prescription is complicated. I'll have to wait until I get home—if Jenn isn't too embarrassed to be seen with me." He touched The Girlfriend's arm.

Seeing Dad like this felt weird. He always was kind, especially to women like Grandmom and Mrs. Mendez, and the moms at school. But it was different with The Girlfriend, like he was an art-loving kid who had discovered a box of a hundred and twenty crayons when all he'd had was the eight-pack.

The Girlfriend smiled. "I'd never be embarrassed to be with you, babe."

"But can you see?" Ava asked.

"More or less," Dad said. "Are you feeling better?"

He stared at her with unusual intensity, as if daring her to confess. His gaze asked not only if Ava felt better, but if she was going to continue fighting this mountain trip. If she was going to continue ruining his perfect vacation with his perfect girlfriend and her perfect daughter.

Ava wiped her hands on her shorts. The sooner they got to the lodge and found out someone else had their cabin and all the other places were full, the sooner they could return to Denver.

"I am feeling better. A little."

CHAPTER 11

It was as dark as midnight early the next morning when The Girlfriend's Jeep merged onto I-70. Despite the hour, cars, trucks, and RVs choked the highway, darting in, out, and across three lanes. To Ava, the endless string of red brake lights screamed **DANGER AHEAD**.

Eventually, the bustle of Denver yielded to an open, shrubby landscape. Compared to humid Iowa with its lush farm fields, Colorado looked dry, rocky, and barren. Plus: flat.

Ava hadn't noticed when exactly the morning had grown light, but now, brilliant bands of orange and pink streaked the sky. Grandmom had taught her to pause and appreciate times like this—she called them a wink from God, little sparks of unexpected beauty or awe that appeared in a normal day. But this felt like a trick. The pretty colors probably came from Colorado's dangerously thin air and closeness to the sun. Normally, Ava offered a thank-you when encountering a God wink. Now, she pleaded silently: Please get me out of here.

Dad turned around. "Who wants bagels?"

Z was still chewing the last of hers when she reached for her new Zorn book. She must have noticed Ava watching, because she said, "So good."

Ava, also chewing, nodded.

"I brought the first one," Z said, "if you want to read it."

Ava pointed at her mouth to show she couldn't talk and nodded again.

Z smiled extra huge. "This is going to change your life for-ev-er!" She grabbed her bag and retrieved a paperback as thick as a Harry Potter novel.

"Prepare to be blown away," Z said. She waited for Ava to finish chewing, swallow, and clean her hands on her napkin before presenting *The Zorn Chronicles Vol. I: The False Mage*. "It'll be confusing at first. Some things don't make sense until book three."

Ava ran a hand over the worn cover.

"It's Rodrigo's," Z said. "He got into them before me. We love the same books."

Ava looked up. "But aren't these for kids?"

"All the best books are. That's what Rodrigo says. I guess it's because kids are still open-minded, and we use our imaginations and stuff. A lot of grown-ups…" Z shrugged, one shoulder higher than the other. "Well, you know."

"Yeah."

The False Mage opened with an elaborate map, followed by a complicated family tree and a glossary for the book's invented language. Ava skimmed the table of contents. Finally, she flipped to the last chapter. For Ava, many stories were too nerve-racking to read without knowing that everything worked out in the end. Instead of ruining the story, this allowed her to relax and enjoy it.

"Stop," Z screeched, making Ava jump. "You can't do that!"

"Don't yell," The Girlfriend yelled. "I'm driving!"

"Ava, what happened?" Dad said.

Ava's thrashing heart had stopped her voice from working.

Z pressed her hands to her cheeks. "I let her borrow the first Zorn book."

"What's a Zorn book?" Dad said.

"The awesomest fantasy series ever. And she"—Z pointed an accusing finger—"is reading the end!"

"Ava's a fast reader," Dad said. "She's a grade ahead in language arts."

This made Z's head explode, practically. "I just gave it to her!"

"Leave Ava alone, Z," The Girlfriend said. "You're not the reading police."

"It's my book."

"I—I am going to read the whole thing," Ava whispered. "From the start."

"You probably shouldn't read in the car, Ava," Dad said. "You might get sick."

Z looked up. "I used to get carsick when I was little."

That was irritating. She was only six months older.

With a sigh, Ava shut the book. Then her heart did a teeny, tiny skip. Because: Colorado had changed again without her noticing. It looked as if a giant had smooshed lumps of clay into irregular, towering humps and then pinched the tops and added grass and evergreens for decoration. Foothills. She couldn't imagine that mountains were larger than this.

Ava had never seen Z so quiet for so long. With the tip of her tongue poking out, she devoured page after page, as if she were starving and the words were cheeseburgers.

It wasn't fair that Ava couldn't read in the car too. She opened Z's book. She would read a couple of paragraphs or a page. A chapter, tops.

After a while, though, Ava stopped sneak-reading and simply read. No one noticed. But as the road grew curvier, Ava began to feel queasy. She shut the book, but the feeling worsened, as if some monster in her brain had shot icky tentacles through her body.

"Look, Ava," Dad said. "Isn't it amazing?"

Ava opened her eyes.

Colossal.

Massive.

Ginormous.

The biggest words weren't big enough to describe the Colorado Rockies. They merged into a solid rock fortress, a zigzagging skyline soaring as far as Ava could see. The largest cast violet shadows across the smallest, which were merely huge. It was surprising how dark green they appeared, thanks to their Christmas-tree coats. Even though it was summer, snow topped some of them, like dollops of whipped cream.

"Amazing," she echoed. And so, so dangerous. At least they weren't going to stay.

The road twisty-twisted.

Ava shut her eyes and breathed.

Goosebumps rose on her arms. What if this icky feeling was altitude sickness? Ava couldn't remember the symptoms. Was *that* a symptom? Confusion was one. Was she confused? More than usual? She yawned. Exhaustion…another symptom.

Ava cracked open her eyes.

The road whipped back and forth, one sharp U-turn after another.

"Holy guacamole," she breathed.

The road looked as if it shot straight off the mountain.

Into clouds.

"Dad?"

Correction: The clouds were *below* them.

"I'm sick."

"We're almost there." He turned and handed her a half-full water bottle.

"I—I need to stop…"

"Can't, Baby Ava Girl."

Ava gritted her teeth. Was Dad in that much of a hurry to get to that dumb cabin? He didn't care if his daughter was sick? Or maybe even dying from altitude sickness? She drained the water. Her stomach sloshed. Then: Black dots. Silver flashes. BlackSilverBlackSilver. Ava dropped the empty bottle and pressed her palms into her eyes. Sparkling silver glitter floated slowly down. Because: Her head was a snow globe.

"Ava? What's wrong?"

Did Dad not understand "I'm sick"?

"Motion sickness," The Girlfriend said.

"Are you going to barf?" Z's shouting mouth was inside Ava's ears.

Z's book levitated magically from her lap.

"Were you reading?" Dad asked.

Ava's head hurt, and something bad roiled inside her. "I need to stop," Ava repeated, covering her eyes. "For real."

"We can't. I told you. There isn't any place to pull over."

What? Wasn't that a law? Ava peered through her fingers. The road skimmed the mountain's edge. There was no shoulder, no safety rail.

Only rocks.

Clouds.

Air.

Spit flooded Ava's mouth.

The Girlfriend said something about fresh air. Dad said something like "relax"—as if that had ever helped anybody, anywhere. Z was going on about hands, windows, fingers. It was all a distant soundtrack, like a movie playing in another room.

Ava's stomach heaved, and she threw up.

Z shrieked.

The Jeep slowed and brakes screeched behind them.

Ava braced for the inevitable crash that would shoot them off the mountain like a Matchbox car tossed by a toddler. But The Girlfriend stomped the gas, and they lurched forward.

No crash. Only a couple of angry honks and The Girlfriend's swear.

Dad stretched over the console between the front seats. "Oh, Baby Ava Girl." His voice was soft. "Shh."

Because: Throwing up always made Ava cry.

She coughed and sputtered and wiped her vomit hands on her shorts.

Dad rubbed her shoulder, and Ava wanted to cry even more because it felt so good. "Hold on," he said. "I'll get some water."

A moment later, Dad leaned back over the seat. "A sip," he warned, handing her a water bottle.

He pulled off his shirt. His chest was the blue-white color of skim milk. He took the bottle back, poured water onto his shirt, and gently wiped Ava's face and hands.

One reason Dad liked working at home was that he didn't have to dress up. This wasn't one of his usual T-shirts, though. It was one of his sporty good shirts, with a collar and pocket.

"I'm sorry," Ava whimpered. The tape on his glasses shattered her heart.

"Shhh. It's okay," Dad said. "Did any get on you, Z?"

"My leg," Z said through the top of her T-shirt, which she'd stretched over her nose and mouth into a DIY gas mask. She shook her extended leg, as if she didn't want it connected to her body. Dad wiped Z's leg with a clean part of his shirt and turned back to Ava. "I need to unbuckle your seat belt—just for a minute."

Before she could protest—surely he'd seen the National Highway Traffic Safety Administration data—he'd undone Ava's seat belt and wiped her shirt and lap. The Jeep turned sharply. Dad braced against the roof, while Ava slid into Z, and Z crashed against her door.

Dad wasn't wearing his seat belt. Neither was Z, who was searching for something on the floor. Ava had read enough news to know how this ended. The highway patrol would say three of the four Jeep passengers had not been wearing seat belts. So they were dead.

"Seat belts," Ava cried, fumbling with hers.

"Ava's right, Mackenzie," The Girlfriend called back. "We're almost there."

Dad took a swipe at the floor with his shirt, patted Ava's knee, and returned to his seat.

The wind felt good against Ava's damp face. The Girlfriend must have rolled down her window.

"Stick your hand out and wiggle your fingers," Z said through her T-shirt mask. "It takes away motion sickness."

Ava thrust her arm out the window but kept it close to the Jeep for safety reasons.

Colorado Road Signs

Stay in Lane

Runaway Truck Ramp

Avalanche Area

Lost Brakes? Merge Left.

In case of flood, climb to safety.

Motorcyclists Use Extreme Caution

Sharp Curves

Wildlife Crossing

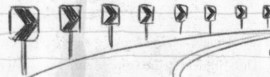

CHAPTER 12

What was taking so long? Ava had changed clothes and brushed her teeth in the women's bathhouse, and Dad, who'd put on a clean shirt, still was trying to check them into their cabin. But: There was no cabin. End of story. Return to Denver.

"I think I got it," The Girlfriend said. She wadded up the wet paper towels she'd used to clean the back of the Jeep and walked to a nearby garbage can. "Have you seen these?" she called to Ava. "They have a special lid to keep out bears."

Bears.

Certain people might be unhappy when they couldn't stay. Really, though, Ava was looking out for all of them.

The Girlfriend settled on the curb next to Ava. "Feeling better?"

"I think so." Ava touched her watch. "I'm sorry for—"

"You couldn't help it, sweet pickle. I'm sorry you've had such a rough time." She touched Ava's knee. "This is a special place for Z and me, and we're excited to show it to you and your dad. We've only stayed in the hotel, though. I've always wanted to rent a cabin."

Ava felt a twinge of guilt. The Girlfriend was nice. But she and Z could stay at a cabin another time—without Ava and Dad.

Z jogged over. "What's taking so long?"

"Something's wrong," The Girlfriend said, rising. Dad strode toward them, scowling, a woman in a green Soaring Eagle shirt behind him.

"Someone has our cabin," Dad said.

Ava's armpits tingled.

"They have to get out," Z said.

"Come here." The Girlfriend gently pulled Z in front of her, wrapping her arms around Z's shoulders. "What do you mean?" she asked Dad.

Z turned to look at her mom. "Rodrigo's coming."

"Shh," The Girlfriend said then looked at Dad. "I don't understand."

"I'm terribly sorry," The Soaring Eagle woman said. "We don't know what happened. The cabin is unavailable." Her necklace name tag said: "Ting, 5 yrs., Beijing, China."

"Another family has it," Dad said, raising his hands and dropping them.

"That's not right," Z said.

"Is there another—"

"Booked," Dad said.

"What about a room?" The Girlfriend continued. "Or—"

"Nothing," Dad said.

"Another hotel?"

"Nope." Dad smiled a tight, thin-lipped non-smile. "We called them all."

"It's our cabin, Mom." Z's voice cracked.

"Hold on, Mackenzie—"

"Tell her," Z said, turning again. "We had a reservation."

"That's what I don't understand," The Girlfriend said, looking back at Ting.

"Someone called and said you couldn't make it," Ting said.

"You called," The Girlfriend said to Dad.

He pushed his broken glasses up his nose. "They think I canceled all ten days."

"But you didn't," Z cried.

Ava bit the inside of her cheek. What if Z remembered her call yesterday? What if she whirled around, pointed at Ava, and said, "She did this!"

"They said they even sent a cancellation email," Dad said.

"You didn't get it?" The Girlfriend asked.

Dad, hands on his hips, shook his head.

"I can book another visit," Ting said. "Give you a discount—"

"They live in Iowa," The Girlfriend said.

"Rodrigo's coming," Z wailed.

The Girlfriend sighed. "Z, I want you to take a walk."

"But—"

"Let the adults figure this out."

Dad glanced at Ava on the curb. "Do you feel well enough to go with her?"

Ava hoisted herself up and headed toward a nearby picnic table. "Don't go far," Dad called. "Watch for cars."

Z stomped after her. "This is idiotic," she yelled. "We should call the police. We should sue!" Stomp. Stomp. Stomp. "Get those people out of our cabin!"

Ava made a concerned face. Inside, she smiled. Her plan had worked even better than she'd dreamed. They would return to Denver soon, and no one would know what she had done.

Ava should have been zooming back to Denver, not hiking.

As it happened, Soaring Eagle Resort had a place they could stay. Maybe.

It was an old hermitage, Dad said, a rustic cabin built for one person—possibly two—who wanted to "get away from it all" to pray and think. Part of the appeal must have been getting extra close to God because, apparently, the hermitage sat high on a mountain.

Walking—actually, hiking—was the only way to get there.

After making sure Ava's motion sickness had passed, Dad attacked her with sunscreen and bug spray, leaving her sticky, stinky, and coughing. Then, with their bags locked in the Jeep, they circled the main lodge to the trail to the hermitage.

Z dashed ahead like usual. Ava didn't know which was worse, that Z didn't realize how dangerous the mountains were or that The Girlfriend let her run off alone.

"She's fine," The Girlfriend said, as if reading Ava's mind. "You can't get lost if you stick to the trail."

"Why are we even looking at it?" Ava grumbled. "It's not big enough."

"No harm in checking it out. Besides," Dad said, grinning, "do you have other pressing appointments this morning?"

Ava sighed. She wasn't in a teasing mood. She tripped and ran a few stumbling steps.

"Whoa!" The Girlfriend caught Ava's elbow. "You okay?"

Behind them, a tree root thicker than Ava's arm edged the path like a snake.

"Be careful, Ava." Dad's playful tone had vanished. "Watch where you're going."

Birds keened in the distance, scolding her too.

"You've got to stay alert," Dad continued. "That's really, really important out here."

As if Ava needed reminding. But the rough terrain was trickier than it looked. Even though they were in the mountains, Ava had heard "trail" and expected one like those at home: flat and paved, perfect for bikes and roller skates.

This trail was a wild thing, a narrow slash of naked earth tearing through dense evergreens and studded with sharp stones and booby-trap roots. It rose and dipped without warning too, causing Ava to trip on nothing at all. The tallest trees shouldered out much of the sun. The shadow world below cradled decaying logs and dead trees, some still waiting to fall. Dry leaves and pine needles, faded to brown but still pointy-sharp, shrouded the ground.

The trail twisted and turned, forcing them up, endlessly up. Ava's legs churned in slow motion. Fought a new mega-gravity.

It was only a quarter mile to the hermitage, but the steep incline and thin air made it a strenuous workout for people who weren't used to it. Ava sometimes joined Mrs. Mendez for her after-supper "constitutional"—a quarter-mile stroll through their small town. Even with a bad hip, eighty-five-year-old Mrs. Mendez covered that in no time. But now Ava panted, her lungs hollering for air even as she gulped it through her mouth.

"Let's stop," The Girlfriend said.

Dad breathed heavily too. He shrugged off his day pack and handed Ava a water bottle. The water was warm but satisfyingly wet, and Ava longed to suck it down. But the memory of drinking so much in the car—then hurling—was enough to make her sip. She couldn't throw up here in the woods, exposed and unprotected.

"I think we're almost there." The Girlfriend wiggled her water bottle back into the stretchy mesh pocket on the side of her pack. "You're doing great, Ava."

"You are, Baby Ava Girl."

Ava had never thought much about him calling her that. Now it was like a pebble in her shoe. How could he not know she'd out-grown babyish nicknames?

They continued, the only sounds their plodding footfalls, random birdsong, and mysterious snaps and rustles deep in the shadows. Despite what The Girlfriend said about sticking to the trail, Ava began to fret that they were lost, when, finally, they crossed a rocky ridge and entered a clearing with a wooden hut.

Z bounded toward them. "What took you so long? Can we fit in there? All of us?"

It was a good question. The hermitage looked smaller than Grandmom and Granddad's shed. But it was not the correct question. Because: It was obvious, even from a distance, that no one should step inside that thing. It looked like the shoddy stick house the lazy little pig built in the fairy tale. No way would they stay.

Encountering Mountain Wildlife

	Black Bear	Mountain Lion	Moose
Make yourself look bigger? (arms up/out)	Yes	Yes!	No!
Eye contact?	No! Bear will take it as a sign of aggression, but keep bear in sight.	Yes! Act like a predator— throw rocks and sticks; wave arms.	No!
Speak in a low, calm voice?	Yes!	No! Make noise!	Yes, slowly back away.
Run?	If need to, run in a zigzag pattern.	No! Don't turn away, either.	If moose charges, try to hide behind a rock, tree, or car.
If attacked	Fight back with sticks, rocks, cooking pan.	Fight back. Protect neck and throat.	If knocked down, curl into a ball to protect head and vital organs. Play dead.

CHAPTER 13

The tilted wooden steps creaked under Dad's weight and the hermitage door swung wide with a tap. "It'll be cozy," he said over his shoulder.

The others followed, with Ava halting on the porch. The hermitage's one room held a narrow twin bed frame without a mattress, a nightstand, a small wooden desk and chair, and a rocking chair—all covered in thick dust. It was far dirtier than Grandmom and Granddad's shed. Even from the porch, Ava smelled something foul, like decaying leaves mixed with wet dog.

"Ting wasn't fooling, huh?" Dad said, wiping his forehead with an arm.

"Where's the bathroom?" Ava called from the porch.

"You get your own outhouse," Dad said. "How fancy is that?"

"Eww. Those are nasty," Z said, but quickly added, "It's just a few days, though."

"That's right," The Girlfriend said, "and the bathhouse by the lodge—" She sneezed.

It sounded like a scream, and made Ava jump. But at least the hermitage didn't collapse.

"Bless you," Dad said. "There's no—"

The Girlfriend sneezed again, and twice more.

"Are you okay?" he asked.

"Allergies." The Girlfriend blew her nose on a tissue from her pack. "Sorry. I was going to say, there are flushing toilets at the lodge and the bathhouse."

Dad looked at Ava. "There's no electricity here, either. Or internet or phone service."

It sounded like something out of a horror movie. But Dad smiled as if he enjoyed imagining how hideous it would be if they stayed, which, of course, they wouldn't. Couldn't.

What if Dad got crushed by a boulder? Yellow "falling rocks" signs had peppered the highway. (If you couldn't pull over to throw up, what good were those warnings?) What if Z was balancing on one leg, fell, and broke it? Even if they could call 911, no ambulance could get up here without roads. This vacation was even more dangerous than Ava had imagined.

"We can't stay, Dad," she said, stating the obvious.

"It's okay," Z said.

"No, really," Ava said.

"It's fine."

"Yeah," Ava said, "it's not."

"The main lodge has phone and internet service," The Girlfriend said, as if that was Ava's main objection. "We'll be down there a lot. They have so many activities."

Dad stepped toward the open door. "Even if we were staying in the other cabin, we'd want to get out and enjoy nature. Right, Ava?" He stared at her. "We'd get out in nature?"

Ava had nothing against nature. In Iowa, though, it didn't try to kill you.

"We can rough it for a few days," The Girlfriend said.

"It might be fun," said Z, obviously sucking up so she could see her one-named dad.

"There's no kitchen?" Ava asked.

"The main lodge has a cafeteria," Dad said, exchanging a quick look with The Girlfriend. "They don't allow food up here."

Ava peered around the door. "How come?"

"Bears." Z's voice was matter of fact, as if she'd said "kittens."

"You can't have anything with a scent up here," Dad said, "like shampoo."

What kind of dumb bear ate shampoo? Of course, Dad hadn't mentioned that *they* were the biggest scented objects in the "cabin." A huge, furry beast grew in Ava's mind. His sharp fangs dripped as he told his buddy, "I was dying for shampoo, but I guess we can go ahead and eat these people, since they're here. That little one with the short hair looks delicious."

Ava swallowed. She had to think this through. She couldn't go inside the cabin because it was disgusting. She couldn't *not* be in the cabin, though. Because: Bears.

"Is that"—Ava stared at the pile of leaves and sticks under the desk—"a nest?"

The Girlfriend jumped back. Dad knelt down and looked at it.

"Hello, Headly family," a cheerful voice boomed from the woods, and, for a second, Ava wondered if the bears had sent a welcoming committee to put them at ease so they wouldn't suspect the attack later. Sneaky. Plus: Only she and Dad were Headlys.

Two young men in resort staff shirts like Ting's strode up the trail, walkie-talkies swinging from their belts.

Z brushed past and leaped off the porch. Ava walked down the normal way.

"Welcome to Soaring Eagle," one of the guys said in the same cheerful voice. He had dark skin and a big, bouncy Afro. His name necklace said, "José, summer, Bronx, NY."

"What do you think of the hermitage?" he asked. "Think you might want to stay?"

He smiled the nicest smile—straight at Ava. Her mind scrambled for a reply.

"It looks like some creature beat us to it," Dad said.

"Oh. Well. Okay." José looked at his partner. "Can't have that."

"Jens, 1 yr., Copenhagen, Denmark" shook his head. Sunlight glinted off his patchy blond whiskers.

"Let's check it out," José said, winking at Ava. Before she could process this—what did it mean?—José's long, muscled legs strode toward the hermitage. The adults followed.

Maybe he'd had something in his eye? But, no. It was a wink. Ava was sure, practically. Her stomach fluttered in a pleasant-unpleasant way. What did *that* mean? His dark eyes were pretty, his lashes long and curly. Those were facts.

"You need to stop," Z whisper-shouted.

Ava stepped back, her cheeks hot. Had she seen the wink?

"Stop trying to make us leave."

"Oh." Relief mixed with anger. Ava had been distracted. Now she was back on track. "We can't stay. It was built for two people at the most. At. The. Most, Z."

"Stop being a scaredy-cat baby."

Ava sucked in a breath. "Scaredy-cat baby" was even worse than plain scaredy-cat. Z, who thought she was so cool because she dyed her hair and had already gone to middle school, strolled away.

"Where is everybody going to sleep?" Ava called, following. She'd taken a big risk to cancel their reservations. Her excellent plan couldn't fail.

Z scrambled onto a boulder and climbed, her hands and feet finding holds in cracks and dark holes in the rocks, perfect hiding places for rattlesnakes and ground squirrels. Z didn't care where they slept or if she put them in danger. Z cared about one thing: Z.

———————————

"They have a climbing wall and a huge pool with a high dive!" Z flipped a page of the resort's magazine. "Horseback riding and night hikes and s'mores." She looked at Ava beside her. "Have you ever played flashlight tag?"

It was rude not to answer. But hadn't Z been rude to her? Even more important: Dad wouldn't want Ava to be rude. She stirred her soup and said nothing.

"It's hide and seek in the dark," Z continued, as if she wasn't a mean, selfish, name-caller. "I bet it's super fun here."

How about super dangerous? In the dark, someone could run right off the mountain. Ava also did not want to climb, swim, dive, hike at night (seriously?), or eat s'mores. That awful hermit-age had ruined everything.

They were eating lunch in the resort's cafeteria, but Z ignored her mac and cheese to study the activities offered that week. "Mom!" She bounced in her seat. "There's a new zip line! You know I've always wanted to do that. Can we? Please?"

"We'll see."

"Maybe we should wait for Rodrigo, though," Z mumbled, as if to herself.

Dad leaned across the table toward Ava. "If your stomach feels better, you should eat." He'd insisted she get clear broth because of the fake sickness yesterday and the very real throw up that morning. "Remember, we can't have snacks up at our camp."

As if she could have forgotten. "I don't want to sleep in the hermitage," Ava said.

"You and I are going to sleep in a tent," Dad said. "Like real camping!"

That sounded worse. "I don't want to be here," Ava whispered.

"I know." Dad put down his bison burger. "I'm sorry you feel that way."

If Ava had even a smidge of natural acting ability, it hadn't come from him. Because: No way was Dad sorry. Not even half a bit. Plus: If he cared about her, they'd have never come. YOU'RE A LYING LIAR WHO LIES, Ava wanted to shout.

"It's not safe."

"Ava, we agreed to table this issue." Dad dragged three french fries through a ketchup puddle and stuffed them into his mouth. He chewed, swallowed. "It's decided."

They'd decided. Stupid Dad, Stupid The Girlfriend, Stupid Z. Three against one.

"Were you listening to Z?" Dad wiped his mouth with his napkin. "All the cool stuff you can do here? We're going to have fun."

"Oh no." Z banged the table. "I forgot my tutu!"

"I brought it," The Girlfriend said, "and mine."

"Rodrigo's my partner—oh!—you don't think he's going to show."

"Did I say that?" The Girlfriend asked.

"He's doing a shoot near here."

"I understand, Mackenzie, but—"

"You don't want me to see him."

"You know that's not true." The Girlfriend's eyebrows bunched together. "I don't want you to be disappointed. You know how unpredictable…his schedule is."

"You don't get it. You're not an artist." Z returned to the lodge magazine.

Part of Ava had still wondered if The Girlfriend was going

to have a baby with Rodrigo. But she didn't sound like someone wanting to get back together. Still, Dad had said he and The Girlfriend were a long way from having babies. None of it made sense. Ava wished she could ask. But "are you having a baby?" and everything the question implied (romance, kissing, nakedness) was way too personal and embarrassing to ask someone she barely knew. Besides, The Girlfriend and Dad probably wouldn't answer truthfully anyway. And Dad had made it clear that he didn't care about her research and opinions.

Z looked at her expectantly. "Did you bring a costume?"

"What for?"

"The Mud Run!" Z looked at Dad as if they were part of a secret gang. "I thought you were doing it."

Dad cleared his throat. "Actually, Baby Ava Girl…"

Ava's eyes screamed: AGAIN? ARE YOU KIDDING ME?

And: WHO ARE YOU?

And: WHERE IS MY REAL DAD?

"The Mud Run is a fun parent-child activity," Dad said. "We're going to have a blast."

It was like he was trying to hypnotize her, constantly telling her how much fun she was going to have in Colorado's deadly mountains.

"You get to wear a costume," Z said.

"They do it every year," The Girlfriend chimed in. "People come from all over."

"I've always wanted to do it," Z said, bouncing again, "and now I get to with Rodrigo!"

"But what is it?" Ava said.

"An obstacle course," The Girlfriend said. "In mud."

Z grinned. "Isn't that off-the-charts awesomesauce?"

Ava stared at her. "It sounds off-the-charts awful," she said. "I'm not doing it."

"Ava," Dad said. "Come on. Don't be like that."

"What's the big deal?" Z asked.

Ava glared at her. "If you spent five minutes researching Colorado instead of watching Rodrigo videos, you'd know." She tapped her watch under the table. "Unless you're stupid."

"Ava Louise," Dad said. "That's enough."

"I didn't say she was stupid. I only implied she *might* be stupid."

Dad stood. "Come on." He took Ava's arm.

His grip didn't hurt, but getting hustled out of the cafeteria in front of kabillions of diners, including Z and The Girlfriend, was embarrassing. Another girl might have screamed, kicked, dropped to the floor, and gone limp in protest.

Ava wished so hard she was that kind of girl.

Instead, she wiggled free of Dad's grip but didn't run. They passed a gift shop, a guest business office, and a snack shop before entering the main lodge. They crossed the cavernous room to a stone fireplace that reached the ceiling.

"Sit," Dad ordered. It was like he was training Mouse, except in that case he would have said it nicer. And given a treat.

Ava sat on one of the oversized leather chairs. Dad took one beside her.

"What's going on?" he said.

Wasn't it obvious? Ava didn't want to do the Mud Run. Still, she'd surprised herself by being so mean to Z.

"I don't want to be here," she said. "I don't want to be with any of you!"

"That's fine." Dad stood. "I'm going to finish my lunch. Do not move, Ava Louise."

Without saying goodbye, Stupid Dad headed back to the stupid cafeteria, leaving Ava in stupid time-out like a stupid preschooler.

MORE COLORADO DANGERS
(extremely partial list)

Wildfires: Flames often look farther away than they really are and can move super fast. Smoke can make it difficult to breathe.

Hypothermia: Body's core temperature gets too low. (Can be fatal. <u>year-round</u>.)

Poisonous plants: Death camas, Purple larkspur, Lupine, Western water hemlock

Avalanches: Colorado often leads US for these deaths. (Only in winter?)

Ghosts: Tourists encouraged to visit <u>real</u> haunted hotels, houses, parks, streets, cemeteries, and a museum in an old prison.

CHAPTER 14

The main lodge was large and airy, with a beamed, A-shaped roof. Employees in green Soaring Eagle shirts stood at a long counter in the back, checking in guests and answering questions. Behind them, real wild animal heads stared down from the wall. A fuzzy buffalo head seemed as big and round as the giant hay bundles Granddad's baler spit out.

There were other chairs near the stone fireplace. People bent over books, phones, or tablets. Others sat at wooden tables, playing cards and board games or working on laptops. One white guy wore a stocking hat—never mind that it was June—and tapped on an old typewriter.

How could Dad have signed her up for something called a Mud Run? The Mud Run, with its different obstacles, sounded suspiciously, horribly similar to Field Day, with its activity stations. But that had been in Iowa, which had enough oxygen and no horrible mountains. This would be a quintillion times worse.

"Hey, there!" José, the lodge employee who'd winked at Ava at the hermitage, walked toward her. "We've got a cleaning crew at your place."

"Oh. Thanks."

"Sure. Hey, do you own a pink backpack?"

Ava nodded.

"You must like to read."

Ava's cheeks warmed as she nodded again.

"Cool," José said. "Me too."

He was going to think she couldn't talk. Ava needed to say something.

"I'm José," he said, tapping his name tag necklace. "My mom named me after a writer."

Ava perked up. "Really? Who?"

"José Martí, a poet and journalist. He fought for Cuba's independence. My grandparents came to America from Cuba."

"Really? Mrs. Mendez—she's one of my best friends—she came from Mexico."

"Cool." José smiled. "And who are you?"

"Oh." She swallowed, her cheeks burning now. Why had she made such a silly comment? Why would he care that she had a friend who had immigrated too? "I'm Ava."

"How's it going, Ava?" They shook hands like grown-ups. José's big palm was dry and warm. "Where's home?"

"Iowa."

"Sweet. I'm from the Bronx. You know it?"

"It's in New York City." Heart pounding, Ava added, "One of the five boroughs."

"You been?"

Ava shook her head no.

"So, tell me," José said, raising his chin and moving his hands to his hips, "how does an Iowa girl who's never been to New York know the five boroughs?"

Ava hid her smile behind her hand. "I did a school report. For extra credit."

"Right on." José raised a hand. "Give me five, Ms. Ava. Best city in the world."

"Then why are you here?" Ava was curious but immediately worried that her question sounded snotty.

"You mean, why did I leave the best city in the universe?"

"Yeah."

José laughed and dropped into the chair Dad had left. "I'm in grad school back home, studying environmental engineering— trying to help save the planet—and they have some great summer programs here, where you can work and learn stuff, and I mean—" His long arm swept the length of the large windows framing evergreens, mountains, sky. "Who wouldn't love that?"

"That's really cool."

"Yeah. But I haven't left the Bronx, not really." He pressed his palm to his heart. "It's always here."

"That's not the same."

"True." José ran a hand over his chin. "It's all connected, though. The Bronx. Iowa. These mountains. Even me and you."

What was he talking about?

"Through energy," José said.

"You mean atoms?"

"Something like that. Have you heard of the energy field?"

Ava shook her head no.

"It's an idea some people have that even though everything looks separate, it's really all connected through energy. I like to imagine there's this big love energy bubbling all around." His dark eyes met hers. "It's like this: *I come from everywhere, and I go everywhere; I am art among the arts; with the mountains I am one.*"

Ava had never heard anyone talk like that. She wasn't sure what he meant. Or how to respond.

"That's part of a poem by José Martí, the writer I'm named after."

"Oh." *With the mountains I am one.* No, thank you.

"I've been thinking about it a lot since I got here," he said with a little laugh. "You got me talking, Ms. Ava." His smile faded. "Hey, you okay?"

The kindness of the question made Ava want to cry.

Because: No, she was not.

José looked around. "Where's your family?"

"Eating." She wanted to clarify that Z and The Girlfriend were not her family, but she touched her watch instead. She expected him to ask why she wasn't eating with them. She wanted to explain, but she didn't want him to think she was a bad person.

In a lot of conversations, people seemed eager to say their next thing. It was easy to sit back and let them talk. But José seemed comfortable sitting quietly.

"I—I said something mean," Ava whispered. "Super mean."

José didn't look shocked or disgusted, which was a relief. "I'm not usually like that," she added. "I was mad, I guess."

"How do you feel now?"

"Bad." Ava's stomach churned. "Still mad."

"Do you know about five, four, three, two, one?" José asked. "It's a game I like to play when I need a little grounding. Like when I'm feeling worried or weird."

"You get worried?" Ava asked. She couldn't imagine he ever felt weird.

"Everybody does," he said.

Not long after José's walkie-talkie squawked and he had to leave, Dad sprung Ava from time-out. Her stomach twisted when they met The Girlfriend and Z on the lodge's front porch. What if they hated her now?

"Ava, what do you say to Z?" Dad said, like she really was a toddler.

Ava and Z stared at each other.

"Sorry."

"Z?" The Girlfriend prodded.

"I accept your apology," Z said.

As they headed back to their camp, Z raced ahead. Again.

It wasn't fair. Z had called Ava a scaredy-cat baby. Of course, their parents hadn't heard. But where was Z's apology? Ava didn't speak during her second mountain climb of the day. She wasn't quiet, though. The effort made her breathing loud. How could Dad think she could do an obstacle race in the mountains—in mud?

Her heart sank when she spied the domed tent beside the hermitage. How could Dad possibly think the filmy fabric would protect them from hungry wild animals and countless other mountain dangers? She thought about the animal heads in the lodge. Their relatives probably were plotting revenge. They'd see the tent as an inconvenience, like a candy wrapper.

At least the hermitage had solid walls and a door. A jar of wildflowers sat on the porch, welcoming them back. Inside, everything had been swept, dusted, or hosed down. Even the slimy leaves/wet dog smell was gone, mostly.

"Who needs a fancy cabin?" Dad said, pulling The Girlfriend close and kissing her cheek.

A mattress now topped the bedframe, and the bed was neatly made—until Z bounced on it. Pillows, sleeping bags, blankets, and deflated air mattresses sat beside it. The desktop held gallon jugs of water and glasses. A battery-operated lantern perched on the nightstand.

Z riffled through a box on the floor, pulling out flashlights, headlamps, batteries, and other supplies. She tossed aside a flyer with the alarming title "Be Bear Aware!"

Ava wasn't quite sure what to do with herself. She stood barely inside the door, her arms at her sides, buzzy and heavy. She felt bad about what she'd said to Z and for her snotty apology. Normally, she would have offered a sincere one.

The problem: That's exactly what Dad wanted her to do. Making him happy was the last thing Ava wanted. In fact, if he was going to force her to stay, surrounded by every kind of wilderness threat, shouldn't she ruin his vacation? She didn't want to be mean, but if everyone had a terrible time, maybe they'd want to leave early. Ava still could hear those gross, slurpy kisses from That Night, could still see Dad and The Girlfriend's candlelit faces mashed together, his hands tangling her hair. If they didn't have a fun vacation, maybe they'd realize a long-distance relationship wasn't the best idea?

Ava imagined a Future Dad, one who was nice again, who didn't keep terrible secrets and wore stylish glasses. He'd thank her for helping him see that breaking up was best for everyone. *What was I thinking, having a girlfriend who lived all the way in Colorado?* he'd say. *Long-distance relationships are super hard and expensive!*

Ava's stomach jerked. Because: What about those pregnancy-test sticks? What if The Girlfriend was pregnant, and Dad was the father? But what about Rodrigo? Like Mouse when he wanted to play fetch, the idea wouldn't leave her alone. At lunch The Girlfriend hadn't sounded like she even liked Rodrigo. But they had loved each other once. They'd had Z. What if someone helped them remember?

Did you hear that The Girlfriend and Rodrigo had a baby? Future Dad whispered to Ava. *They're back together, and everyone is happy!*

The Girlfriend sneezed. Loudly.

"Bless you," said Dad, the real one.

Ava waited, and, sure enough, she sneezed three more times.

As Z and her mom made plans to swim, Dad turned to Ava. "You should take it easy, make sure you're fully recovered."

She nodded. "Can I please use your phone?'" She missed Kylie and Emma so much.

"Sorry." Dad squinted at the screen. "No service."

5, 4, 3, 2, 1 from José
(named after a writer!)

Think to yourself or whisper:

5 things you can see right now,

4 things you can touch,

3 sounds,

2 smells,

1 good thing about yourself.

Helpful for worries, weirdness, and times you feel like your head is floating away.

CHAPTER 15

That evening, Ava ate a burger without getting another time-out. But despite her leisurely afternoon—Z's Zorn book was getting good—she could barely keep her eyes open. The sun burned overhead but it felt like midnight, as Ava trudged with The Girlfriend to the women's bathhouse. Z skipped ahead then circled back like an annoying fly.

"It's the altitude," The Girlfriend said, holding the bathhouse door open for Ava. "You'll feel better soon."

Inside, The Girlfriend tapped the code on the locker where they'd stored their shampoo, toothbrushes, and other personal, scented things that weren't allowed at camp.

Ava shuffled into a shower stall like a sleepwalker. Z's bare feet were visible in the next one. No shower shoes for her. Just germs.

Later, Ava wasn't sure why they'd bothered. Each ponderous step back up the mountain raised a dusty cloud that settled on her once-clean self.

When they finally reached camp, there was a new conundrum: It was too early for bed, but Ava was dead tired.

"Maybe you could sleep in the tent," Dad began, "and I…"

Ava crossed her arms and narrowed her eyes. No way was she sleeping in a tent alone—on a Colorado mountain—while Dad hung out with The Girlfriend and Z in the hermitage.

"I guess we'll see you in the morning," Dad finally said. "Oh, I almost forgot." He pulled a bottle of allergy medicine from his pocket. "A little gift."

"Thanks, babe," The Girlfriend said. "That's sweet."

When they kissed, Ava stalked to the tent. When Dad entered soon afterward, she pretended to sleep.

"Sweet dreams," he said, kissing Ava's forehead.

But, of course, sleep was impossible.

It was too light. Strange shadows drifted like ghosts across the thin walls and ceiling. Sometimes the wind jiggled the tent poles. If a pole hit her head, Ava could get a concussion.

It was noisy too. The rush of the wind sounded surprisingly like crashing ocean waves, a sound Ava knew from visiting Dad's parents in Florida. Insects clicked, chirped, and buzzed, and birds whistled, tweeted, and trilled, each trying to be loudest. There were troubling, unidentifiable sounds: "err-err-errerr," "chirchirchir," "ah ah ah," "eee-eee," and a sound that reminded Ava of sloppy gum chewing. (Was that Z? From inside the cabin? Except: It wasn't allowed up here.)

"Try to relax, Baby Ava Girl," Dad whispered when he finally shut off the lantern. "You've got to get some sleep."

As if she were awake on purpose.

"I don't want to mud run," Ava said into the dark. "It sounds a lot like Field Day."

"What do you do when you fall off a horse?"

Ava groaned. She'd always thought that saying—get back in the saddle—was strange. Maybe it was smarter to avoid horses altogether?

"You can do it," Dad said. "You're strong, Ava."

But Ava wasn't, and Dad's lie only made it worse.

———————————

The next morning, Ava woke with one overpowering urge. "Dad! Dad!" She jostled his shoulder. "I have to go to the bathroom!"

He opened one eye. "You know where the outhouse is, don't you?"

"I can't go by myself!" She danced in place. "Hurry!"

"Hold on." Squinting, he reached for his glasses, sat up, and wiggled a tennis shoe onto his bare foot. Ava realized she should do the same.

The sky was lightening but the sun hadn't risen when they set out.

"Dad," Ava shouted, "did you have a good sleep?"

"Shh." He glanced back at the hermitage.

"But, Dad," Ava continued. "We're supposed to make noise so the wild animals STAY AWAY!" She scanned the shadowy trees, praying she didn't see shiny eyes staring back.

"A normal tone is fine, Ava."

"BETTER SAFE THAN SORRY!"

The outhouse, which stood just off the trail, looked like a little house. When it came into view, Ava ran. She yanked the heavy door—and found a normal toilet! This wouldn't be so bad.

Skylights near the roof allowed in some light, but the room darkened considerably when Ava shut the door. Plus: It smelled weird. Ava held her breath and cautiously approached the toilet. With the tips of her index finger and thumb, she lifted the lid.

It was not a normal toilet.

The urge to pee was so strong now, it hurt. But, safety first: Ava covered the seat with toilet paper. But the TP was cheap single-ply. Ava added another layer.

When she finally perched on the edge of the prepared seat, WHOOSH! A mysterious gust of cold air burst out of the hole and straight up onto Ava's exposed parts. The air pouring out of the toilet hole was grocery store freezer aisle cold, raising goosebumps on Ava's arms and legs.

And then a truly horrific idea occurred to her: If air was flowing out of the hole, did that mean snakes and other animals could do the same? One sharp butt bite from a plague-infected ground squirrel could kill her. Ava finished her business and hurried out of there.

"Z and I thought it'd be fun to go horseback riding this morning," Dad said, leaning forward and cupping his coffee mug. "Is everybody in?"

Ava poked her pancakes. She did not want to balance on a big, wild horse that might gallop right off the mountain. But that didn't stop a left-out pang from blooming in her chest.

"Ava?" Dad said.

"No, thank you." She rubbed her watch under the table.

"I'd really like you to come," he said. "You can't stay by yourself—"

"Actually, Eric?" The Girlfriend set down her coffee. "I don't think I'm up for it, either."

Dad looked surprised, and that made Ava happy. Because: He didn't seem to have a problem with her staying by herself in stupid time-out yesterday.

"Me and Rodrigo are going to dinner tonight!" Z rocked in her chair, waving her phone.

"Don't shout," The Girlfriend said, glancing at neighboring diners before turning back to Dad. "I'm not feeling well."

"He's picking me up at six!" Z whisper-shouted. "He texted me yesterday, but I just got it. I hate not having Wi-Fi."

Dad looked at Ava. "Have you ever been that excited to see me?"

"I doubt it."

Dad chuckled, but Ava wasn't sure she was joking.

"I'm sorry you're not feeling well," he said, taking The Girlfriend's hand. "Do you need to see a doctor?"

"It's my allergies."

He nodded and looked at Z. "I guess it's you and me, cowgirl."

"What should I wear?" Z said. "Tonight, I mean. With Rodrigo, you have to be prepared for anything."

Once they left, The Girlfriend smiled at Ava. "What time is it?" she asked, then groaned, and lightly swatted Ava's arm. "You need to fix that watch!"

Ava stiffened. Her fingers found her watch, which was fine as it was.

"I'm sorry," The Girlfriend said. "I...There's a bracelet-making class. That's why I asked." She checked her phone. "It starts in ten minutes. Does that sound fun?"

"Okay," Ava said.

They crossed the road and followed a flower-edged sidewalk a short distance to the resort's arts center, a boxy, wooden building embellished with bright, abstract designs. Seconds before they reached the door, a ground squirrel burst out of some nearby bushes.

Ava screeched and jumped.

The Girlfriend yelped and grabbed Ava's arm. "What?" She looked around as if expecting to face the zombie apocalypse.

The twitchy little rodent had disappeared.

Ava didn't answer until they were safely inside. "Ground squirrel."

"What?" The Girlfriend looked back as if at least one zombie had slipped in behind them.

"They carry plague," Ava said.

"They want you to feed them," The Girlfriend said, "which you definitely should not do. And don't try to pet them, either. But they won't hurt you, Ava. Just ignore them."

The Girlfriend caught Ava's eye, the way Dad did when he wanted to make sure she was listening. She sounded like Dad too.

CHAPTER 16

Ava's insides jittered from the ground squirrel sighting long after she and The Girlfriend found seats at a table in the sunny craft room. Two older women sat across from them and said hello. One wore a visor and the other had a slash of red lipstick on her front tooth.

The art supplies, neatly labeled and arranged on white, open shelves, looked like something out of Grandmom's decorating magazines.

"Do you like art?" The Girlfriend asked.

"Yeah," Ava said, "but I'm not very good."

"Same," The Girlfriend said. "Z is the artist in the family."

"She said you helped with her room."

"Yeah, well." The Girlfriend sighed. "I won't do that again."

"Why?" Ava had secretly sort of hoped, maybe, that The Girlfriend might visit Iowa someday and make her room awesome too.

"There were whole days we didn't speak."

"Really?" Z and her mom fought a lot. Maybe Colorado made it hard for them to get along, like it was doing to Ava and Dad.

The teacher introduced herself as Abigail, a college student from Falls Church, Virginia, working at the resort for the summer. She rolled her wheelchair among the tables, delivering supplies. Everyone received a hand towel, a straight pin, three eco-friendly hemp cords, and some beads. Abigail demonstrated how to tie the cords together and anchor the knot to the towel with the pin.

"We'll braid them about one-third of the way," she said.

Ava pinned her cords and started to braid. "Z's excited about dinner with Rodrigo tonight." She tried to sound casual. "How did you guys meet?"

The Girlfriend blinked. "Rodrigo and me?"

"Yeah. Was he already famous?"

"No, no, no." The Girlfriend laughed, but it wasn't happy. "I knew him when he had a last name and no money."

"All right," Abigail called to the class. "Next, we'll need to add the beads." She demonstrated how to thread a cord through a hole in the bead and work it into the braid.

Ava wasn't there yet. Plus: Her braiding looked lopsided. She unraveled the cords.

"The bead part seems harder than it should be," The Girlfriend muttered. She'd added one, but there was a strange hole in her bracelet. "I was a ski bum," she said, sliding off the bead to begin again too. "When I met Rodrigo."

Ava looked up at her. "What's a ski bum?"

"Someone who lives and breathes skiing."

"You must like it." It sounded super dangerous.

"Loved it. I still do. I was working at a ski resort over winter break, and when it was time to go back to college…"

"What?"

The Girlfriend rolled a bead between her fingers. "I didn't."

Ava couldn't imagine such a thing. She didn't know it was legal. "You left…to ski?"

"I went back eventually and graduated. At the time I wasn't sure what I wanted to do."

"Did Rodrigo work there too?"

"No." The Girlfriend chuckled. "He was on vacation with friends. He was trying to ski, I guess." She smiled. "He's not a skier—at all. But we hit it off, and he stayed."

"What do you mean?" Ava pushed a cord through her first bead.

"He worked at a newspaper—he's older than me—and he called his boss and quit. I wouldn't call it a responsible thing to do," The Girlfriend said, but she didn't look unhappy.

"That's romantic."

"It was. And foolish. A bit of foreshadowing, unfortunately."

This did not seem like a good part of their story to follow. "What was he like?"

"Have you seen him on TV? Is that why you're curious?"

"This isn't right." Ava tried to smooth her bracelet. "This sucks."

"I'm sorry. I didn't think this would be so hard."

"I haven't seen his show," Ava said, steering the conversation back where it belonged. "I'm interested because he's Z's dad, and she says he's amazing."

"She adores him."

From The Girlfriend's tone, it sounded like Z might have been the only one. "Have you heard of divorced people getting remarried?" Ava plunged her pin all the way into the towel, then plucked it out with her fingernails. "I read a newspaper story about it—"

"What?"

"Lots of people do it." Ava moved the pin in, out, in, out. She felt The Girlfriend's stare. "They work out their problems, the stuff that made them get divorced, and—"

"Ava—"

"Then they're really happy. And the kids are super happy. I'm sure Z—"

"Ava, I'm with your dad! You know that, right?"

Ava's cheeks exploded in fire. Did The Girlfriend think she was stupid? She ran her fingers over her bracelet. It was lumpy, and not only because of the beads. "This is horrible," she mumbled.

The Girlfriend leaned in to look at Ava's bracelet. "Yours is better than mine." She pushed hers toward Ava.

"Yours isn't bad," Ava said. "I mean, it's not hideous."

They laughed.

One of the women across from them, the one with the lipstick on her tooth, turned to the other. "Can you imagine us making bracelets with Mother?"

"Absolutely not," the visor-wearing one said, and the two giggled.

"It's so nice to see a mother and daughter getting along," Lipstick Tooth said.

"Oh," The Girlfriend said. "I'm not her mom."

The older women exchanged a look. "You're definitely related," Visor Head said.

"The resemblance is there," Lipstick Tooth agreed.

Ava looked up.

The Girlfriend smiled. "They thought I was your mom."

Ava hadn't realized the women had been talking about her. Except for their blonde hair and light skin, she and The Girlfriend didn't look alike. (And The Girlfriend was a darker blonde.)

"Maybe she's a favorite aunt?" Lipstick Tooth suggested.

They seemed to be hinting that Ava should tell them how she knew The Girlfriend. It was a simple question with an easy answer. But Ava's chest grew hot. Her hand moved to her watch.

The Girlfriend put her arm lightly around Ava's shoulder. "We're friends," she said, giving Ava a small squeeze. "I have a daughter the same age, and, you'll notice, she's not here."

"Well," Visor Head said, "isn't that always the way?"

The grown-ups chuckled and returned to their bracelets. But an uneasiness rustled inside Ava. Maybe those strangers were trying to be nice or find something to talk about, but it was none of their beeswax what was going on between Ava and The Girlfriend.

Plus: What was going on between them, exactly?

A tornado rose inside Ava, and she stood. Unsure what to do with herself, she wandered to the counter that held large spools of bracelet cords. Ava's eyes fell on a bin holding several small, clear plastic containers. She picked one up.

It gleamed in the sunlight.

Kylie had once told her about a prank at camp. Some older kids had poured glitter onto the blades of a ceiling fan in the mess hall. "Most of us had no clue," Kylie said. "But someone turned on the fan at lunch—instant sparkle storm!"

Ava and Dad's tent didn't have a ceiling fan, of course, but maybe she still could prank him? She headed to Abigail. "Could I have some of this?" Ava whispered. "I could pay for it. I'd like to make my dad a birthday card."

Abigail didn't need to know his birthday was months away.

"That's so sweet. Let me see if I can find something to put it in."

The Girlfriend was bent over her bracelet.

Abigail returned with a plastic sandwich bag. "Will this work?"

"Perfect," Ava said. "Thank you so much."

"Do you need construction paper too? Or a glue stick?"

"Oh, no. Thanks. I forgot the glitter. This will make it so special for him."

Ava stuffed the bag of glitter into her pocket and returned to the worktable.

"Is everything okay?" The Girlfriend asked.

Ava looked at Lipstick Tooth and Visor Head. "She's The Girlfriend." Ava's voice sounded flat, loud, and strange.

The women looked up. "Beg your pardon, dear?" Visor Head said.

Ava swallowed. "She's my dad's girlfriend."

"They're visiting from Iowa," The Girlfriend said.

"How nice," Lipstick Tooth said with a puckered smile.

"Except my dad has tons of girlfriends." The lie flowed like the sweet maple syrup Ava had poured on her pancakes that morning. "When things get serious, he dumps them." She raised her hands. "It's a whole thing. Did you know you have lipstick on your tooth?"

When they left the art center, Ava looked for the ground squirrel that had ambushed them earlier. Fortunately, it was gone. But that didn't relieve her stomachache.

"Is something wrong, Ava?" The Girlfriend asked as they neared the lodge. "Are you unhappy about your dad and me?"

Ava's hands balled into fists. She wasn't used to talking about sensitive topics.

José, her favorite resort employee, stood on the front porch with a clipboard. A small group of adults, many with walking sticks and poles, stood nearby. It looked as if José was about to lead them on a hike. Although Ava wasn't necessarily a fan of hiking, she was tempted to run and join them just to escape The Girlfriend.

"I'm sure it's weird," The Girlfriend continued as they started on the trail to the hermitage, "visiting a new place and seeing... seeing your dad"—she made a laughing sound that wasn't a laugh—"with somebody."

Ava's fingertips tingled. She shook her hands.

"Z's been unsure about Eric. It's nothing against him—"

"I know," Ava said quickly.

"Watch out!" The Girlfriend steered Ava around a rock jutting from the dirt path.

"I saw it."

With a sigh, The Girlfriend ran a hand through her hair. "In the class, when you said I was your dad's girlfriend, you sounded…"

Ava bit her lip. Saying mean things had become her Colorado hobby.

"Let's stop a minute," The Girlfriend said.

Ava bent over to catch her breath. Colorado had made her a liar—and mean. A mean liar who'd hurt someone. But even if she'd known how to fix it, she couldn't. Wouldn't.

She needed Dad and The Girlfriend to break up so everything could be normal again. Even if they weren't ready for babies, if they kept seeing each other, eventually they might be. The Gross Kissing Night, seared into Ava's brain, was proof of that. If Dad and The Girlfriend got closer, Ava didn't know how her life might change.

"In the future, it's probably best to discuss those things in private," The Girlfriend said. "And you can always ask me anything, Ava. Okay?"

Ava nodded.

But she did not ask: Do you hate me because I'm mean?

She did not ask: Are you pregnant?

She did not ask: Is Dad the father?

"Being in nature really calms me," The Girlfriend said as they resumed walking. "Can you tell me why you're so unhappy to be here?"

Ava licked her lips. "I'm really thirsty."

"We'll be there soon." Ava felt The Girlfriend's stare. "Can you tell me what's wrong, Ava? Maybe I can help." The only way The Girlfriend could help was to get them back to Denver now. Or make the mountains not be the mountains. And stop talking. "If I could understand what you're feeling, what you're scared of—"

"I'm not scared." Ava's voice was strangely loud. "I'm not feeling anything!"

CHAPTER 17

When they arrived back at camp, Dad and Z were still out riding horses. The Girlfriend kicked off her shoes by the hermitage door and headed for the bed. "I need to rest," she said.

Ava was glad. She craved alone time but no way was she going to stay in the tent by herself, at least for very long. Reading in the hermitage while The Girlfriend napped would be the next best thing. "I'll be right back," she said.

Ava rumbled down the front steps, scanned for wild animals, and dashed to the tent. She glanced around. How could she prank Dad? His sleeping bag caught her eye. Ava unfurled it, poured in the glitter, shook it, and rolled it back up. She grabbed Z's Zorn book on her way out.

As Ava approached the hermitage, another idea struck her. She stopped and scooped up a handful of pebbles and dirt by the steps.

She was pleased to find The Girlfriend resting on her side, facing the wall.

Ava crouched, set down Z's book, and, as quietly as possible, poured the rocky dirt into The Girlfriend's tennis shoes. She shook the debris into the toes. When The Girlfriend put them on, she'd get an unwelcome surprise.

They were silly pranks. But anything that made their vacation a little more unpleasant might make them want to leave. Plus: Ava couldn't bear to witness another make-out session.

———————————

The Girlfriend glanced at her phone. "He's late," she said. "You're sure it's tonight?"

"Yes, I'm sure." Z twirled around one of the lodge's front porch columns. "Jeez."

She wore a tank top, leggings, and booties, all black, and she'd traded her stud earrings for big, silver hoops. Her lips were shiny too. She looked very grown-up.

Ava hoped Rodrigo arrived soon. She was starving.

"Did you thank Eric for taking you to ride horses?" The Girlfriend asked.

"Thanks, again." Z peered around the column at Dad. "It really was fun."

"My pleasure," Dad said. "You're quite the equestrian, Z. Next time, we'll have to get these two to join us." He reached for The Girlfriend's hand.

He and Ava had been in the tent when The Girlfriend put on

her shoes in the hermitage. She hadn't said anything when they'd met at the trail. She hadn't even walked funny. He'd be mad if he knew what Ava had done.

"Rodrigo!" Z shouted as a sleek black car pulled into the circle drive. She turned to her mom. "See?"

He was an hour and a half late.

Z's face fell, though, as a woman got out of the car. "I'm so sorry," she called, jogging up the steps. She was older than Dad and The Girlfriend, a white woman in jeans and a girlish ponytail. "Hey, Z! Great to see you again!"

"Where's Rodrigo?"

"He's meeting us there."

The Girlfriend stood. "Is he finished for the day? Absolutely finished? You're sure?"

"Mom," Z wailed.

"I don't want you waiting for him," The Girlfriend said. "Again." She introduced Dad and Ava to Penny, Rodrigo's assistant.

"They have the site for twenty more minutes," Penny said. "It can't go longer."

Z headed to the car.

"Z?" Penny called. "Rodrigo wants you to bring your friend."

Ava's stomach dropped. Did that mean her? Rodrigo wanted her to come?

Z looked briefly confused, as if she didn't have any friends here. "Why?" she asked.

"I don't know if that's a good idea," Dad said, rubbing the back of his neck.

"He doesn't even know her," Z said.

"Z wants to spend quality time with her dad," Dad said.

It was like they were performing a spoken-word poem.

"Actually," Penny said. "Rodrigo insisted."

Dad frowned.

"She'll be okay," The Girlfriend whispered. She smiled at Ava. "I'm sure you'll have lots of fun."

"I'll watch after her," Penny told Dad.

He still looked doubtful. "Do you want to go, Ava?"

Ava wiped her hands on her shorts. She wasn't wearing anything cool like Z. But even if she'd known ahead of time, she didn't own anything cool. She'd never eaten with a celebrity. More important, though, this was a chance to get The Girlfriend back with her ex-husband.

"Yeah. I want to go."

Ava joined Z in the back seat. "I'm excited to finally meet him," she said.

"Yeah." Z turned toward her window.

Didn't she want Ava to come? Z had talked nonstop about how great Rodrigo was and how Ava had to meet him. Plus: Rodrigo wanted her to come. Ava had no idea why, and Z didn't seem up for discussing it. Or anything.

As the car snaked along the curvy roads, Ava breathed deeply and touched her watch. Maybe it was good her stomach was empty. The last thing she wanted was to throw up. Again. Finally, Penny turned into a gravel parking lot next to a small building with a glowing sign that read "Al's Place" and showed two beer bottles clinking together.

"Is this a bar?" Ava whispered. "Are we allowed?"

Al's Place was dark, cramped, and nearly empty. It didn't look like the sort of place where Ava imagined someone rich and famous would eat. A baseball game blared from a couple of wall-mounted TVs. A few old men leaned over drinks at the wooden bar. A smattering of other people sat at mismatched tables and chairs around the room. They stared as Penny led the girls across the oddly sticky floor to one of several empty booths. Ava slid in first, her shorts catching on peeling duct tape.

A cheerful, blue-haired woman placed a basket of peanuts on their table. "Welcome to Al's. I'm Meg, your server, bartender, cook, and Jill-of-all-trades."

She handed each a one-page, laminated menu. "The peanuts are free—toss your shells on the floor," Meg said. "The burgers are good. The pizza is frozen. I'll give you a minute and be right back with water."

Now that they'd left the twisting roads, Ava's hunger had returned.

"When's he coming?" Z's jiggling leg rocked their bench.

"Soon," Penny said. "We should order, though."

"You make a great burger," Ava said as Meg cleared their plates.

"Thank you, sweetie. Can I get you anything else?"

"How about a father?" Z said.

"Sorry, hon," Meg said. "All out."

The bar had filled up—mostly with young women. "Look at all the people," Ava said. "It was dead when we got here."

Z frowned. "They know," she said.

"Know what?" Ava asked, scanning the room again.

"He's coming."

As if on cue, a man who could only be Rodrigo entered the bar, looking exactly like the picture Z had shown Ava that first day. He was shorter than Ava had imagined, though, especially given Z's height. He wore tight black jeans, cowboy boots, and a button-down shirt that revealed a thick gold chain and tattoos.

Ava grabbed Z's arm. "Is that him?"

Rodrigo approached with an easy, loose-limbed stride. "Z! Where's the love, girl?" He opened his arms, and Z rose to give him a half-hearted hug. He kissed both her cheeks and stepped back, hands on her shoulders. "Look how tall you are. And so pretty." He glanced at some people who had come in with him and taken the neighboring booths. "My genes, eh?" They chuckled and murmured agreement.

Z didn't smile. "We were supposed to have dinner, Rodrigo."

Rodrigo slid onto the bench beside Ava, leaving Z standing.

"How's it hanging, Ava?" His smile vanished. "I hear your dad's seeing my wife."

Ava's stomach tightened. She glanced at Z for help, but she was looking away.

Penny reached across the table and swatted Rodrigo's arm. "Don't tease," she said.

Rodrigo laughed. "Aw, I'm messing with you, kid," he said.

Ava laughed with relief. Talk about a good actor.

"I didn't mean to give you a heart attack. Lo siento mucho." *I'm really sorry.*

"Está bien," Ava said. *It's okay.*

"Whoa!" Rodrigo threw up his hands and turned toward her. "¿Hablas español, Ava, mi amiga?" *Do you speak Spanish, Ava, my friend?*

Ava's cheeks warmed. "Solo un poco." *Just a little.*

She was excited to take Spanish next year. But she'd picked up a lot from Mrs. Mendez over the years.

"Está bien," Rodrigo said. "Did you know when two people speak Spanish together, they become friends for life?"

"Did you make that up?" Ava asked, laughing.

"This one—" Rodrigo gestured at Z and shook his head. "Ella no habla español."

Z didn't speak Spanish. Ava wasn't sure if Rodrigo was saying she couldn't or wouldn't. Either way, it sounded bad.

"Did you know she's great at riding horses?" Ava asked.

"Is that right?" Rodrigo pushed up from the table. "Excuse me, ladies. We need to get this party started." He sauntered to the middle of the small room. "Drinks on me," he hollered.

Everyone cheered.

"You okay?" Ava whispered as Z rejoined her in the booth.

Z shrugged, one shoulder higher.

They hadn't known each other long, but Ava had never seen Z this quiet, at least when she wasn't reading. The way she'd talked about Rodrigo, Ava had expected Christmas, Disneyland, her birthday, and the Fourth of July, all together.

He returned and sat across from Z. "I can't believe how tall you're getting."

"You said that."

A young woman hovered nearby. Rodrigo didn't seem to notice. "How's school?"

"It's *summer*, Rodrigo."

"Oh. Right."

"Summer *vacation*."

Ava looked at Penny. Should they give them some privacy?

Rodrigo nodded. "How's your summer going then, Miss Thang?"

"Gee, Rodrigo." Z spit the words. "I'm having the bestest summer ever!"

He exhaled. "She's taught you well," he mumbled into his drink.

"I'm not my mother," Z said.

"Excuse me, Rodrigo?" The hovering young woman inched closer and waved. "Hi."

He smiled. "Hi."

She giggled. "Hi."

Ava looked at Penny and back at Z. What was happening?

"I'm a huge fan, and I'm passionate about photography." The woman pushed her hair from her eyes. "Could I possibly steal you for a second? I'd love to pick your brain."

"What's your name?" Rodrigo asked.

"Cassie. Cassie Kennedy. It's such a thrill to meet you."

"Cassie Kennedy." Rodrigo shook her hand. "Superstar name right there." He raised his chin at Penny. "I'll just be a minute."

Rodrigo grabbed his drink and headed to a dark, empty corner with the fan.

Z shot out the door.

Penny ran after her.

CHAPTER 18

Penny was supposed to watch them, but she'd left with Z. Now Ava sat alone in a Colorado bar. Should Ava have run after Z too? If so, what was she supposed to say? Ava felt bad for Z, but did Z even care about Ava?

Rodrigo remained in the corner with Cassie Kennedy. More young women had joined them, surrounding him. Apparently, the word was out: The photographer/judge from *Make Me a Top Model* was at Al's Place, and every superfan and aspiring model in the Rockies needed to meet him. (As well as people who liked free drinks.)

What if one of the old men at the bar offered Ava candy or said they had a puppy to show her? Those were tricks criminals used to snatch kids. Puppies reminded Ava of Mouse. She'd never been away from him so long. What if he'd forgotten her? She ran a finger over her watch.

It wasn't fair her mom died.

Dr. C. wanted her to notice and name her emotions, but that assignment made Ava mad, upset, and worried. Because: How was she supposed to know?

Did other people just know?

Was "bunched up" a feeling? What about "twizzled" or "bumpy"? The words for feelings weren't big enough to hold them.

If her mom were alive, Ava wouldn't have been sitting alone in a mountain bar.

In this moment, Ava felt so many things: sad, twitchy, angry, swirly, shocked, fearful, curious, shaky, confused, grumpy, doubtful, clammy, disappointed, lonely, tense, sweaty, weary, suspicious, edgy, fluttery, trapped, itchy, rattled, vomit-y, bummed, sore, ignored, nervous, hopeful, tingly, bored, queasy, irritated, tired, jumpy, abandoned, and unsure. She wasn't even sure all of those *were* feelings—or if that was a complete inventory of everything she felt.

Ava's feelings eventually would change. But Ava's mom still would be dead.

Always and forever.

And that sucked.

Ava buried her head in her arms on the table and shut her eyes.

"Hey." Rodrigo tapped her shoulder. "You all right, kid?"

Ava looked up. She wanted to say: Do I *look* all right?

She nodded.

Rodrigo took the seat across from her and looked around. "Where's Z?"

Ava wanted to say: You're a grown man. You caused this. Can't you figure it out?

"She left."

"Left?" Rodrigo pulled out his phone and typed. "They didn't leave you, did they?"

Ava assumed Z was outside, blowing off steam. If she'd wanted to leave, surely Penny would have come in for her. Unless she forgot…

"Would you mind?" A smiling young man held out a paper and pen, and Rodrigo scribbled his single name. A couple more fans approached.

"Uh, sorry." Rodrigo looked frazzled as his phone pinged. "Maybe later, okay?"

He held up the screen for Ava to read:

Rodrigo: Where R U?
Z: U SUCK!!!!!!!!!!

"Is she having her period or something?"

"Uh…" Ava had wanted to know too, but it was a crummy thing for a dad to say. Rodrigo also had said something mean about The Girlfriend when Z was snotty. He didn't seem eager to have a baby with his ex-wife.

But Ava had to try. She took a breath. "I heard about how you met Jenn. How you quit your job to be with her."

Rodrigo squinted. "She told you that?"

Ava cracked a peanut. "I think she wants to get back with you."

Rodrigo threw back his head and laughed.

Ava ate her peanuts, chewing carefully. This wasn't the time to choke.

"No offense, Ava." Rodrigo wiped his eyes. "But I don't think you're reading that correctly." He leaned forward. "And, of course, there's your dad."

"They're going to break up," Ava said. "I mean, I think so." She crumbled the dry, papery shell between her fingers and let it slip to the floor.

"And why is that?"

Below his nonchalance, Ava sensed interest. Maybe he didn't want to be with his ex, but that didn't mean he liked that she was with someone else.

"The way she talks about you," Ava said with a tiny shrug. "Her eyes light up."

Rodrigo looked doubtful.

The truth: That's how Dad looked at The Girlfriend sometimes.

A single streetlight glowed in the Al's Place parking lot, which was now full. Beyond that: a darkness that swallowed mountains.

Ava squeezed her bare arms. With the sun down, it was beyond chilly.

"Z?" Rodrigo yelled. "Come on. I'm not playing."

Ava looked for the car and quickly found it. In the front seat: two dark silhouettes. "Rodrigo? I think they're in the car."

"The car?" He looked confused.

Ava led the way. Rodrigo opened the front passenger door and peered in. "Having fun?"

Arms crossed, face blank, Z ignored him.

"Oh, it's like that?" Rodrigo said.

"Rodrigo—" Penny began.

"No." He held up a hand and then turned to Z. "That's how it is? Okay. See you."

Z leaped from the car. "We were supposed to have dinner," she yelled. "Just us."

Rodrigo wheeled around. "On Monday—*Monday*, Z. I set aside that whole afternoon and night. But you weren't here."

Penny got out and went to stand by Ava.

"That wasn't my fault," Z said.

Ava touched her watch. It was hers. She'd faked being sick on Monday.

"I can't motor up here whenever I feel like it, Rodrigo. I don't own a car. I don't have a license. I'm twelve." She paced a few steps and turned. "Why didn't you send Penny to get me?"

"Where would you have stayed? I'm *working*, Z."

"You're always working. We were supposed to spend time together and you were talking to that—that *fan* who has such a *passion* for photography."

"What do I always tell you, Z? You need to be more patient. Ava and I had a great chat. Didn't we?" He nodded at Ava. "But you were having your pity party in the car."

He put a hand on Z's shoulder. "I know the fans can be a little annoying. Believe me, I know. But they bought your fancy phone. They are part of my work, Z, a big part."

Z stepped back and crossed her arms. "Whatever."

"It's time for Penny to take you back."

"What? No! Rodrigo! It's not even nine!"

After all of that, Z wanted to stay?

Rodrigo ran a hand through his hair. "I've got to get some rest."

"Aren't you at least coming?"

"Can't." He opened one of the back-seat doors, and Ava scooted in.

"Can you give me a hug?" Rodrigo asked Z.

She trudged into his arms.

"I love you," he whispered, kissing her cheek.

Z got into the car.

"One more thing." Rodrigo leaned on the open door. "I can't do that run."

"The Mud Run?"

"Yeah. Sorry."

"Rodrigo, you promised!"

"I'm sorry."

"Please?" Z's voice cracked. "We'll have so much fun."

"I have to work," Rodrigo said with a small shrug. "Buenas noches, Ava." *Good night.*

"Good," Z screamed. "I didn't want to do it with you anyway!"

"Watch your fingers," Rodrigo said, slamming the door.

Z hunched toward the window, her back to Ava.

"I'm sorry," Ava whispered.

Penny started the car and pulled onto the highway. There were no streetlights. Their headlights sliced the black nothingness.

"He's been under a lot of pressure. I know that's no excuse." Penny cleared her throat. "The shoot isn't going well. He really was excited to see you."

Z's sniffles were her only reply.

Ava felt bad for Z. Bad that she couldn't mud run with Rodrigo, bad about the whole miserable night, and bad that she'd caused Z to miss supper with her dad on Monday. But if this meant they wouldn't do the Mud Run, Ava also was glad. That was another weird thing about feelings—how could you feel two opposite emotions at once?

For example, Ava liked Rodrigo. There was something magnetic about him. But he was kind of a jerk.

"I knew it." Z's voice was low. "I knew there was a reason he wanted you to come."

Ava's stomach fluttered. "Why?"

"He wanted me to bring a friend"—Z sniffed and wiped her nose with her hand—"so I wouldn't be alone."

Ava's heart broke for Z. Plus: Did she really think Ava was her friend?

Dad vs. Rodrigo

	Dad	Rodrigo
Great hair	—	✓
Tattoos	—	✓
Rich	—	✓
On TV	—	✓
Hangs with models	—	✓
One name	—	✓
Famous	—	✓
Gave daughter fancy phone	—	✓
Calls daughter embarrassing nickname	✓	—
Super cool but kind of jerky	—	✓

CHAPTER 19

"Wake up." Ava jostled Dad's shoulder. "We've got yoga."

He'd insisted Ava choose something for them to do together. The lodge advertised several options, including rock climbing, golf tournaments (mini and disk), and archery (probably not fun even before someone got an eye shot out). For her forced family fun, Ava had picked the only indoor activity on Thursday: sunrise yoga.

Even better: It was the one Dad seemed least interested in.

He groaned and burrowed into his sleeping bag. "You're sure?"

"If you don't want to," Ava said, "I can stay and read."

"I'm getting up," Dad said, not moving.

"We had so much fun last night," Ava said, dressing in her usual shorts and T-shirt. "Rodrigo is awesome!"

Dad sat up.

Ava turned away. She couldn't watch.

"What—what's this? Ava?"

Ava breathed deeply. If she had any acting talent at all, now was the time to show it off. Slowly, she turned. She put on a confused face and walked over to Dad. "It looks like glitter."

"I know it's glitter. How—how…" Dad swiped at his lower legs and feet, sending glitter everywhere. It stuck to his hands. He wiped them on his shorts, and now they gleamed. He ran his hands through his hair, which wasn't the best choice. "How did it get in my sleeping bag?"

Ava gently bit her cheek. An actor couldn't lose control. "Did you do crafts last night?"

"No, Ava! I did no crafts!" Dad unzipped his sleeping bag and made a strangled sound. "Look at this! Did—did you do this?"

"That's really weird." Ava walked to the door of the tent. "We don't want to be late."

———————————

Ava and Dad arrived early, but people already were arranging mats on the polished wood floor and stretching. An older woman, her gray dreadlocks contrasting against her smooth, dark skin, smiled as they entered. "First time?" she asked.

How did she know?

"Mats are in the closet," she said, pointing.

"Thanks," Dad said.

Ava saved their place beside the friendly woman, who was dressed in a tight, metallic body suit. She looked like a cool superhero.

Ava wished she'd packed her leggings. They usually were too

hot to wear in the summer, though, and she hadn't known she'd be taking her first yoga class in Colorado.

Dad arrived with their mats. "You're sure you want to be here, Baby Ava Girl?" He looked longingly toward the back.

"Of course." Ava always sat in the front row for classes. She didn't want to miss anything. Normally, Dad knew this. Colorado had made them strangers to each other.

Ava certainly wasn't herself. In Colorado she'd become a mean, lying, glitter-bombing machine. She couldn't wait to go home and get back to her kind, truthful self who only used glitter for crafts, and sparingly.

The room began to fill. No one wore plain shorts like Ava and Dad. One guy sported wide, brightly patterned pants, gathered at the ankles, the crotch reaching his knees. His white skin was tan, and his blond hair sat on his head in a bun. Ava had never seen a guy wear a bun, and she liked it. His companion, a tall, thin Asian woman, looked as if she were wearing a fancy bra. Her leggings were covered with holes, not because they were old, but because they were made that way. A white woman about Dad's age wore a sleeveless vest with its hood pulled up and colorful leggings with a little skirt tied at the waist.

Ava unrolled her yoga mat. It was soft, spongy, and slightly sticky. She glanced behind her and her heart sank. She was the only kid. Were kids even allowed?

"Good morning!" someone boomed outside the room. Ava's heart leaped, and she bounced slightly. Because: She knew that cheerful voice! Dad looked at her quizzically.

José strode into the room. His name tag necklace bobbed against his broad chest, which was covered in a stretchy tank top.

"I'm José from the Bronx, and where is that, Ms. Ava?"

Ava's cheeks warmed. "New York City," she whispered.

"Yes!" José walked over to smack Ava five. "I'm so glad to see so many of you here," he continued. "This is your time. For the next hour, I want you to try to let go of the beautiful world out there"—he waved toward the mountains through the wide windows—"and whatever's happening here"—he tapped his forehead. Some people chuckled.

"For an hour, we're going to focus here." He pressed his hand flat to his heart.

José took a couple of steps toward Dad and Ava. "If you feel comfortable slipping off your shoes," he murmured, "we generally practice with bare feet."

"Oh," Dad said. "Sorry."

"All good." José scanned the room. "Let's stand up and feel our feet on the floor."

Dad raised his eyebrows at Ava. They said: I can feel the floor any time. We should be shooting out our eyes at archery. Plus: He hadn't gotten all the glitter off his feet. Or his legs.

"You'd be surprised how many people go about their business twenty-four-to-the-seven and never feel their feet, never sense the support the Earth offers," José said, gliding among his students. "Let's move into *Tadasana*, Mountain Pose."

Ava jerked to attention. She wouldn't have come if she'd known yoga had anything to do with mountains.

"Mountain Pose may seem passive, but don't be fooled," José said. "It's active—using every muscle—and it's the foundation for all the standing poses and full inversions."

Ava looked at the woman beside her, then scoped out the students behind her. Everyone was standing. Was that it? All of it? Was Ava already accidentally Mountain Posing?

Dad gave Ava another look. This one said: Are you kidding? It's regular standing.

And: I had a lot more fun riding dangerous horses with Z.

José approached. "Ms. Ava," he whispered. "Can you lower your shoulders?"

Ava hadn't realized how scrunched up they'd been. It felt good to let them drop.

José smiled. His dark eyes were so pretty. He smelled good too, like fresh, green plants. It felt good to be near him, and Ava found herself smiling.

Then she felt Dad's laser stare, and her cheeks caught fire.

"Shoulders are down and relaxed," José called to the class. "Shoulder blades gently pull together, opening the chest."

He nodded at Ava and moved over to Dad. "Press into the floor while lifting up through your crown. Good. Relax your jaw." José's voice was low.

"Hip bones should be neutral, not up or down," he said louder.

When José moved on, Ava didn't dare look at Dad. She wanted to laugh so badly.

"Some people live in their heads so much, they don't feel their bodies at all." José made his way to the front. "What we're called to do here and now is to pay attention, to simply notice. Let's notice the body. Let's notice the breath. Let's notice Monkey Mind." He glanced at Ava. "That's when your thoughts chase each other like silly monkeys leaping from tree to tree."

Ava had never heard of Monkey Mind. Did her thoughts do that?

For the rest of the class, they stretched and breathed. When Dad couldn't reach his toes, José said Dad should honor where his body was today and breathe "into" his knees. Breathing was super important in yoga.

The second they left the rec center, Dad turned to Ava. "How do you know that guy?"

"José?" Was he serious? "You met him when we first looked at the hermitage."

Dad scratched his cheek. Stubborn bits of glitter dotted his face like shiny freckles.

"You told him about that nest," Ava prompted.

"That was him?" Dad laughed. "I didn't recognize him. Or, I guess I wasn't expecting him to be a yoga teacher too." He stared at her. "You seemed to know him, though." It sounded like an accusation.

"Kind of." Ava gave a small shrug, but her face burned. They headed down the sidewalk to the cafeteria to meet Z and The Girlfriend for breakfast. "We talked at the hermitage a little and in the lodge, when I—when you made me sit there."

"It seemed like, maybe…" Dad rubbed his neck. "You had a crush on him or something."

"Dad!" Flames raced up Ava's neck and scorched her cheeks. "I don't—I—he—"

Dad raised his hands. "It's okay, Ava. Of course, he's too old for you." He laughed—a weird choke-y sound. "Crushes are normal for…young ladies."

"Dad!" Ava covered her face and stopped. She couldn't walk like that—so dangerous.

"Ava." He touched her shoulder. "Jen and Z are waiting."

Ava dropped her hands. Heat whooshed through her. Anger, again.

She did not have a crush on José! Though, if she dated someone in the future, she'd want them to be like him: Smart, poetic, beautiful, a reader, and working to save the planet. But Dad, of all people, should not act like crushes were weird or complain because, maybe, he felt uncomfortable for five minutes. How did he think Ava had felt every single second of this entire trip? Especially on Make-Out Night?

The only good thing was: If Dad was uncomfortable, Ava's plan was working.

Nadi Shodhana Pranayama

(José wrote those words, inspired by the original Sanskrit!)

Also called Alternate Nostril Breathing

1. Use fingers to gently close right nose hole while inhaling through left nose hole.
2. Switch and close left nose hole and exhale through the right nose hole.
3. Inhale through the right nose hole.
4. Repeat.
5. Reduces anxiety, improves well-being. (You're supposed to hold your fingers a special way, but it's too complicated to write.)

CHAPTER 20

Z and The Girlfriend already were seated in the cafeteria. Ava sat beside Z. "Hey," Ava whispered. "You okay?"

Their parents kissed hello. "Is that glitter?" The Girlfriend dabbed Dad's cheek.

"It is," he said, taking a seat. "What do you all know about that?"

"What do you mean?" The Girlfriend asked.

"What do you know about glitter in my sleeping bag?"

Z grinned at Ava. "That's awesome."

Ava's stomach fluttered as she waited for The Girlfriend to tell everyone she'd taken a bag of glitter from the art room yesterday.

"I'm hungry," she said instead. "Should we get our food?"

When they returned to the table, Dad returned to his new favorite subject. "Someone at this table put glitter in my sleeping bag." He sounded irritated.

"You don't know that for sure," The Girlfriend said.

Was she protecting Ava? If so, why?

"Who else could have done it?" Dad said.

"It's a mystery," Z said, perking up. "We should look for clues."

She'd been so upset last night, but maybe she'd moved on?

"Yoga was really great," Ava said.

Dad pointed his bacon at The Girlfriend. "Was it you?"

The Girlfriend laughed. "Are you serious?"

"You sound guilty." Dad crunched his bacon.

"Guilty of what?" She looked at Ava and Z as if they might be in on it. "Pranking you?"

"Is that what it is?"

"I don't know." The Girlfriend sounded annoyed now. "I didn't do it."

Ava risked a look at The Girlfriend, whose eyes screamed back: YOU KNOW I SAW YOU WITH THAT GLITTER BAG YESTERDAY, RIGHT?

"Must have been a bear," Dad said. It would have been funny, except he sounded mad. What a baby! His girlfriend wasn't complaining about the rocks in her shoes.

Ava pretended to wipe her mouth with her napkin. Really, she hid a smile.

The Girlfriend touched his arm. "Are you really upset? About a little glitter?"

"It wasn't a little." Dad stabbed his eggs. "I suppose you're going to say you don't mind me wearing glitter, like you don't mind the broken glasses?"

"Babe." The Girlfriend leaned into him and squeezed his arm.

"I love you in glitter and broken glasses. I love you however you are—even grumpy."

That got a small smile.

They focused on their food until Ava, of all people, broke the silence with an announcement. "Rodrigo's really great."

The Girlfriend offered a neutral smile. Z nodded. Usually this was one of her favorite subjects. She must have still been mad, at least a little. Ava didn't blame her.

Ava turned to The Girlfriend. "He was asking about you."

Z's head jerked up. "He was?"

"He said how funny it was when he tried to impress your mom with his bad skiing." Ava imagined this was true.

"That was funny," The Girlfriend said.

"Who's up for the zip line tomorrow?" Dad asked.

Was Dad changing the subject on purpose? "There's glitter on your ear," Ava said. "The other one."

"You have to sign up a day in advance," Dad said. "Jenn? Ready for adventure?"

"Sorry." The Girlfriend blew her nose. "I'm still not feeling 100 percent."

"If that allergy medicine isn't working," Dad said, "we can try another one."

"I'm sure it'll kick in soon. I bet Z would like to do the zip line, though."

"For sure," Z said, but she didn't sound as eager as the first day, when she'd talked about doing it with Rodrigo. "What about you?" Z asked Ava.

"No, thanks."

Dad looked at The Girlfriend over his coffee mug. "We could wait until tomorrow."

"Then you'd be signing up for Saturday, and that's the Mud Run." She smiled at Z. "We need to figure out our strategy." Apparently, they were partners now. "Sign up today," The Girlfriend told Dad.

As they left the cafeteria, The Girlfriend took Dad's arm. "You know what you need?"

"What do I need?" His lips twitched as if he were trying to mask a smile. Their glitter-inspired grouchiness had passed, and now they sounded…flirty, which was gross.

"Croquet!" The Girlfriend jogged down the sidewalk, pulling Dad. They headed to a field where the lodge people had already set up stakes and wickets for the game. "Come on, girls!"

Ava was glad Z didn't run ahead. "How are you?" Ava asked.

"Fine."

"Really?"

"It is what it is." Z jumped over a sidewalk crack. "Did he really ask about my mom?" She turned, faced Ava, and walked backwards, which wasn't safe at all.

"Yeah." But only because Ava had mentioned it. She didn't want to talk about that. She needed to find out if those sticks hidden in the bathroom were Z's. "Last night, when you were outside, Rodrigo made this joke, like, maybe you were cranky because you had your period."

Z groaned and turned to face the same direction she was walking. "That's so…ugh."

"I know."

"Really sexist."

"Yeah."

"I haven't even gotten my period," Z yelled. "He doesn't know that?"

An old couple stared as they passed. Even so, Ava felt oddly relieved. She'd listened to Kylie and Emma talk about getting their periods, while she still hadn't. It had been embarrassing too, when Dad stocked their bathroom with supplies.

If Z hadn't had her period yet, those sticks were not hers. The theory had been a long shot, and Ava was relieved Z wasn't having a baby. But that meant The Girlfriend was. Maybe.

They were almost at the field. Their parents had chosen mallets. The Girlfriend had blue, which was Ava's favorite color.

"Have you gotten your period yet?" Z asked, just like that.

If Ava told the truth, Z might think she was even more of a baby. "This past year."

Z nodded. "I don't really care. It's not a big deal."

"Yeah."

Except: Ava had lied about it. Z hadn't had her period yet, either. Why would she think Ava was a baby for not having hers?

It didn't make sense, but that's how Ava felt.

Since arriving in Colorado, it seemed as if Ava had forgotten how to tell the truth.

Or even what the truth was.

If she didn't stop, what kind of person would she become?

After croquet, Ava and Dad walked to the lodge so she could use his phone. "I'm going to sign us up for the zip line and then check out the lodge's library," he said. "Get it? *Check out.*"

"I get it."

"You sure you don't want to zip line?" He raised his eyebrows. "Okay. I'll be back soon."

Ava sunk into the "time-out" chair with Dad's phone. Kylie answered on the first ring. "Ava! How's it going? Why haven't you called? Emma and I are dying! Tell me everything! You're probably having a blast with Mackenzie and forgot about us, didn't you?"

Hearing Kylie's voice was like exhaling when Ava hadn't known she'd been holding her breath. She had to laugh at all the questions, though. Kylie sounded like Emma—or Z.

"I've missed you guys so bad." The words made Ava's throat hurt. "It's sort of hard to call when you don't have a phone and there's hardly any Wi-Fi."

"Denver doesn't have good Wi-Fi?"

"I'm not…I'm in the mountains."

Kylie gasped. "Are you okay?"

Ava sighed. "Not really."

"Oh, Ava. I'm sorry."

Ava swallowed. "Hey, were you guys able to go over to Mrs. Mendez's?"

"Yeah, the other day. She was really surprised. It was fun."

"Oh, good." Ava usually watered Mrs. Mendez's plants and

weeded her garden. She'd asked her friends if they could fill in while she was gone. "Thanks for doing that."

"Sure. It was something to do, you know? We played with Mouse and ate those gingerbread piggy cookies you're always raving about."

"Oh, marranitos," Ava said. "Yum."

"So, what have you been doing?"

"Did Mrs. Mendez mention bowling? If they did well, they might be in first place now."

"She didn't say. Are you having fun?"

"Well, Z and I went to a bar last night."

"A bar? You're kidding! Who's Z?"

"Oh, sorry. That's Mackenzie. Have you seen *Make Me a Top Model*? Her dad's the photographer. We—"

"Wait. Back up. *Rodrigo* is Mackenzie's dad? 'Superstar, going far' Rodrigo?"

Kylie knew who he was? "Yeah."

"Emma will die. She'll fall down and die. She loves him too."

"Really?" How had Ava not known this?

"If you see him again, can you get us autographs? Please?"

"Sure. I'll try."

"What's he like?"

This was what Z dealt with all the time. "He's…nice."

"What's wrong? Don't you like him?"

"Yeah, but he and Z had a fight." Ava didn't want to talk about Rodrigo. "Guess what? I put glitter in Dad's sleeping bag. I got that from you."

"Ha!" Kylie said. "Is he sparkly?"

"Extremely. But he's mad."

"Really?" Kylie sounded surprised.

"Honestly? He's been kind of a jerk." Ava's heart sped up. "We're staying in the mountains for ten days, but he didn't tell me. You know how dangerous they are! And he's making me do this Mud Run thing, which is pretty much Field Day with mud and no air."

"Oh, wow, Ava." Kylie exhaled. "That's a lot."

It was a lot a lot, as Z would say. Too much.

"I don't want to be here," Ava moaned.

"I'm sorry. The Girlfriend isn't mean, is she? Do you like her?"

"No. I mean, yes, I like her. She's not mean…" Ava lowered her voice. "She's pregnant."

"What?"

"I don't know for sure. Maybe not. He said they weren't ready for babies, Kylie!"

"If she's pregnant, they might get married. I don't want you to move!"

"I'm not moving!" Ava's heart thudded in her ears. "Don't say that."

"Sorry—"

Ava took a breath. "I haven't been very nice to some people."

"What do you mean? Who?"

"I broke Dad's glasses and made Z miss time with her dad." Ava was going to cancel their zip line reservation that evening too, while pretending to go to the restroom during supper. "I kind of called Z stupid. But she called me a scaredy-cat baby! And just about everything out of my mouth has been a lie. I've sort of…" Ava shut her eyes a moment. "Turned bad."

"Ava Louise! Have we been friends since before we could crawl?"

"Yeah."

"Do I know you as well as anyone does?"

"Of course."

"Okay, then, do you know what I know for sure? You're a good person, Ava."

"I—" Tears pricked behind her eyes.

"When I lost my tooth at Frank's Market and we never found it, you wrote to the tooth fairy to vouch for me. And last year, when LucyAnn stole my cat necklace, you walked right up to her and told her to give it back—and she did! You're a good person, Ava."

"Used to be," Ava whispered.

"Nope. Stop. You've known Mrs. Mendez all your life too. Do you know what she told me and Emma? That you've got a good heart, and she's right, Ava, you do. That doesn't disappear because of one crummy week, a few fibs, and some glitter."

Was Kylie right? Was Ava's heart still good?

"You're in the mountains! Dealing with hard stuff. It's okay to feel what you feel."

Fat tears leaked under her eyelashes. Dad browsed a rack of travel brochures. How long had he been there?

"Dad's here," Ava whispered, wiping her eyes.

"Talk to him. You have a right to know what's going on. Oh! You're going to be a big sister!"

"Maybe," Ava cautioned. "I have to go."

"Your good heart is still there, Ava. It'll tell you what to do."

CHAPTER 21

After supper, Dad, The Girlfriend, and Z wanted to go to the community campfire. "We can't walk back in the dark," Ava said. Why was it always up to her to keep them safe?

"We've got headlamps," Z said. "And flashlights."

"It won't get dark for a long time," Dad said.

They crossed the street from the lodge. The spicy smoke smelled like Iowa in the fall.

"I'm going to make s'mores," Z said, dashing toward the bonfire.

Ava glanced at Dad. His eyes said: Get out of here so I can be on a sort-of date.

Ava's eyes replied: Spoiling your date is my *job*.

"Why don't you go find Z?" Dad said.

He wrapped his arm around The Girlfriend's waist and pulled her close. If Ava hung around, there might be lip-locking. Nobody should have to witness that. Again.

Ava headed toward the fire. Bright dancing flames rose from a pile of logs in a dirt pit circled by rocks. Several people roasted marshmallows on mini metal pitchforks provided by the lodge. Others used wire clothes hangers. Z was already roasting four jumbo marshmallows on a stick. "I'm doing two for you," she said when Ava joined her.

"That's okay," Ava said. "I sort of like mine rare." Even though she stood a safe distance from the fire, the heat warmed her arms and legs. Every once in a while, an electric spray of orange sparks shot into the sky, fizzled, and died, like fireworks.

"Whoa! Whoa!" Z shouted, laughing.

A boy had squeezed between them, and Ava stepped forward to see around him. Z waved her stick like a torch, her marshmallows blazing.

"Z!" Ava shouted. "Stop! Don't shake it!"

The boy hurried away as Z blew on her marshmallow inferno.

Once the flames were doused, she held a protective hand under the charred, dangling blobs as she jogged to a picnic table the resort had set up with supplies.

"Help," Z said. "Hurry!"

Z swayed side-to-side as Ava snapped a graham cracker and topped each half with chocolate. Z used another cracker to rake the blackened glop from her stick.

"You sure you don't want one?" Z took a huge bite. Marshmallow goo coated her lips, cheeks, and fingers.

"That's okay." The burned bits could cause cancer, maybe. Plus: gross. And what if a sick ground squirrel had sneezed on that stick? Ava nibbled her raw s'more. "Um, Z?" This was an important teaching moment. "Did you think about how you could have burned someone?"

Z took another bite and stared at Ava.

"I know you'd never mean to, but you could have touched that boy with your burning stick and caught his clothes on fire."

Z turned. "Who?"

"Or when you waved it around, what if boiling-hot, flaming marshmallow hit somebody in the face? That could cause a serious burn. Or, if it went in that boy's eye…"

"What boy?"

"Him." Ava pointed. "He was beside you. I think you scared him. If you got marshmallow in his eye, that would really hurt. He might go blind."

Z turned back to Ava, frowning. "How would my marshmallow get in that kid's eye?"

"You were flinging it. You—"

"Ava," Z said, pushing the last bite into her mouth, "are you, like, thirty?"

Z thought she was mature!

"Seriously." Z licked her fingers, smacking her lips. "You didn't want to go horseback riding or sign up for the zip line."

Ava's stomach sank. Z hadn't been complimenting her maturity.

"Do you ever—and I mean ever, Ava Headly—do you ever have fun? Even a little bit?"

Fire swept through Ava, scorching her chest, neck, cheeks, the back of her knees. She wanted to respond. But her words were ash.

"Or, let's start with this." Z meanly arched an eyebrow. "Do you even know what fun is?"

Without waiting for an answer, Z dashed into the crowd.

"I know your mom's pregnant. Maybe," Ava whispered to herself. "I know it's dangerous to run with sticks."

Across the way, Dad and The Girlfriend sat in lawn chairs and talked animatedly. What topics made them so excited? After a while, Z joined them. Last night, in the car with Penny, she'd called Ava a friend. Was this how Z treated her friends?

Finally, Ava trudged back to the group.

"Hey." Dad grabbed her hand and pulled her toward him. "Where's my s'more?"

Once again, Ava was in no mood for his jokes. "Can we go?" she whispered in his ear.

"She didn't roast her marshmallows." Z jabbed an accusing finger at Ava.

Dad tilted his head. "Why not?"

How Ava liked her s'mores was her own business. "Can we go?" she repeated.

"Pretty soon." Dad glanced at the Girlfriend and then back. "Hey, Baby Ava Girl?" He was trying extra hard to sound casual.

Ava gripped her watch.

"We were talking, and—" Dad's eyes found The Girlfriend again, and slipped to Z before returning to Ava, who, apparently, was the last to know every single thing. Had Z told on her? But what could she have said? That Ava cared about fire safety and was, in Z's opinion, no fun?

"You know the Mud Run?" Dad said. "Do you mind if Z and I are partners?"

"What?" Ava felt a rush of happiness.

Dad licked his lips. "You know, Rodrigo—"

"I don't mind." Ava couldn't say it fast enough. "That's fine. Totally."

She didn't have to do the Mud Run! If she wasn't so tired, she might have jumped up and down. Maybe her Colorado bad luck finally was turning. No Mud Run for her!

"Have *fun*," Ava added with her own mean glance at Z.

"Ava," The Girlfriend said, "would you please be my partner? I bet we could give these two a run for their money."

Ava looked from The Girlfriend to Dad, her heart thrumming. No! She didn't want to!

"We still have two tickets," Dad said. "It'll be a good chance for you and Jenn to get to know each other better." He lowered his voice. "Got to get back on that horse, right?" Ava's stomach lurched. Did Z and The Girlfriend know about Field Day?

The Girlfriend smiled, though, and Ava felt grateful that she didn't seem to be holding a grudge after bracelet class.

"Come on," Dad said. "It's mud! It'll be fun."

Fun.

Ava hated that word.

———————————

Ava and Z barely spoke the next morning before Z left with Dad to catch the shuttle to the zip line. Z, who thought she was the

Queen of Fun, had no idea she wouldn't be speeding down the zip line, though. It served her right.

It was too hot to be inside the hermitage or tent, so Ava and The Girlfriend spread a blanket under a shady tree, hoping to catch the light breeze. Lying on her stomach and propped on her elbows, Ava tried to read Z's Zorn book. Her eyes kept returning to the same paragraph, though, and she'd gotten confused about which characters were good or bad.

Stretched on the blanket, The Girlfriend soon fell asleep. She was always tired.

Ava's stomach churned. Dad and Z should have been back by now.

She woke to a slamming, banging sound. Ava sat up. "What was that?"

"Hmm?" The Girlfriend was still mostly asleep.

"I heard something." Ava looked for wild animals.

Dad entered the clearing, huffing, his face red and sweaty.

"Hey!" The Girlfriend sat up. "How was it? Where's Z? What's the matter?"

"She must be inside."

The Girlfriend and Ava scrambled after him. Z curled on the bed, a pillow over her face.

"Hey, what's wrong?" The Girlfriend sat beside her and touched her shoulder. "I didn't know you were back." She looked at Dad. "What happened?"

Z sat up and tossed the pillow aside. "We didn't do the zip line."

"Why not?" The Girlfriend asked.

"No reservations." Z looked at Dad.

"I made reservations." His voice bounced off the walls of the small cabin. "What's wrong with these people? I made a reservation."

"I hate this place," Z said.

"What are you talking about," The Girlfriend said. "You had s'mores last night. We've got the Mud Run tomorrow."

Dad sat in the rocking chair. "We rode the shuttle for forty-five minutes."

"And then they wouldn't let you do it?" The Girlfriend said.

Dad shook his head. "Every slot was booked."

"Why didn't they check your reservation before you got on the shuttle?" Ava instantly regretted her question. Because: She sounded guilty.

Dad didn't seem to notice. "Yeah," he said. "They just told everybody who was there for the zip line to get on the shuttle."

"We had to watch everyone else," Z moaned, "until another shuttle took us back."

"And it broke down." Dad laughed bitterly.

"No!" The Girlfriend said.

"Yes." Dad removed his glasses and rubbed his eyes. "We had to wait—"

"On the side of the road," Z said. "For thirty minutes. It was so hot, we were cooking."

"That's awful." The Girlfriend hugged Z and kissed her temple. She got up and went to put her arms around Dad's shoulders. "I'm so sorry." She kissed his cheek.

"I made the reservation," Dad said.

"No one said you didn't," The Girlfriend said.

"The zip line people said I didn't!"

Ava didn't like seeing Dad and Z so upset. But a tiny part of her was glad. She hadn't imagined they'd have to go all the way to the zip line course, and she couldn't have predicted the shuttle breakdown. But they hadn't been in danger—they had plenty of sunscreen and water. And Ava had successfully blocked their *fun*.

"I want to go home," Z wailed.

The Girlfriend turned back to the bed. "You don't mean that."

Dad stood with his water bottle. "Anybody need a refill?"

"Yes, please." Z passed him her bottle.

Dad walked to the desk. "Jenn?" His voice sounded strange. He held the allergy medicine he'd bought. The plastic seal was intact. The Girlfriend hadn't taken the medicine. She'd lied to Dad.

"Oh." The Girlfriend hurried over. "Eric, I—"

"If you don't like this kind or if it's not working, I told you, I could—"

"I know." She touched his back. "Thank you. It's just…"

"I don't understand."

"I don't feel comfortable taking medicine." The Girlfriend's voice turned brisk. "I should have said something. I'm sorry."

"I don't see what the big secret was."

"I said I'm sorry, Eric."

"I'm going outside," Ava said. "It's too hot in here."

She didn't want to be some wild animal's afternoon treat. But she couldn't stand another second inside. No one was acting like themselves: Z was gloomy, The Girlfriend snappy, and Dad had lost his sense of humor.

"I'll go too," Z said, as if she'd forgotten their fight.

Ava was tempted to say something mean. Like: You want to be with me in the no-fun zone? But Z looked so hot and miserable, she didn't.

"This is the worst vacation ever," Z grumbled once they were outside.

Holy guacamole.

Ava's plan really was working.

She hadn't stopped Dad from hauling her to Colorado. She hadn't stopped the four of them from coming to the mountains and then staying. But she had stopped them from having a good time. Because of that, Z hated the resort and wanted to leave. Dad and The Girlfriend probably were close to realizing a long-distance relationship was too hard.

Suddenly, Ava realized: She'd survived an entire week in Colorado!

She was happy. Not *happy* happy. Satisfied, maybe? Content.

Why, then, did she feel sort of rotten?

CHAPTER 22

The heat was unusual for the high country, The Girlfriend said, and they'd all feel better after a swim. Lots of people must have had the same idea. The pool was crowded, with parents bobbing babies in the clear water, kids shouting and splashing, and teenagers sprawling on beach towels, flirting. With its fountains, soaking tower and two diving boards, it was the biggest, fanciest pool Ava had ever seen.

Z rocked on her toes, waiting for Dad to slather sunscreen on Ava's back. Ava tugged at her pink one-piece, which seemed baby-ish next to Z's acid-green bikini. The Girlfriend wore a one-piece too, under a flowy cover-up that prevented Ava from seeing her belly. Dad, in his baggy swim shorts, looked even whiter than usual in the bright sunlight.

When he finally finished, Z said, "Let's play follow-the-leader."

It was a terrible idea, especially if Z was the leader. But Ava didn't want another lecture about her epic un-fun-ness. She followed Z past the shallow end, along the full length of the rectangular pool— straight to the line for the lower diving board.

Ava stopped.

Z skittered back, earning a lifeguard's warning whistle. "You've done diving boards before, haven't you?" Z asked. "In swim lessons?"

"I didn't take lessons."

Z gawked. "You know how to swim, don't you?"

"Yes!"

"But you never had lessons?" Z's right eyebrow rose as if she found this suspicious.

"Grandmom taught me. In her pond."

"Really?" Z looked intrigued. "Don't they have pools in Iowa?"

"Yes." Ava crossed her arms. "We have cars and electricity too, Z."

Z laughed. "If you know how to swim," she said, tugging Ava's arm, "it won't be a problem. It's fun."

The word buzzed between them, like a neon sign.

"Um…" Z swallowed. "I shouldn't have said that yesterday. I'm sorry."

"It's okay." They'd both said and done mean things. Maybe that's why Ava allowed Z to pull her toward the diving board. Plus: Ava knew how to swim.

"Is it nasty to swim in a pond?" Z asked as they joined the line. "Isn't the bottom squishy mud and stuff? Do the fish bite? Do you think the Loch Ness Monster is real?"

Although Ava's nerves were jangly—after all, she was about to go on a diving board for the first time—and even though her feelings still felt tender from the night before, she laughed. Ava had never met anyone who hopscotched through interesting topics like Z. "When the fish nibble, it tickles. Sometimes the plants are scratchy, though. And, yes, there's mud." Wasn't Z the one who was excited about the Mud Run tomorrow? Tomorrow. Urgh.

"What about"—Z giggled—"fish poo?"

Ava smiled. "Swimming in fish poo is the best, Z!"

Z laughed.

Ava motioned toward the shallow end. "Half those little kids already peed in the pool."

Z laughed harder.

"More than half," Ava said. "Eighty-three percent."

"You know what, Ava? You're funny."

"Funny" wasn't the same as "fun," but it was nice.

"You're funny too, Z."

"I was third-funniest in my class last year."

Ava was about to ask how Z knew her rank, when a chubby kid ahead of them in line turned toward them. "You two doing the Mud Run?"

"Sure," Z said. "Are you?"

"Third year," he said. "Are you ready?"

"Dude." Z crossed her arms and popped her hip. "I was born ready."

He laughed. "You've heard about the Tower of Doom, I suppose?"

"Of course."

Ava's throat went dry.

"It gets to first-timers," the boy said.

Had Z kept this important info from Ava on purpose?

The board made an echoey thunk-thunk as a girl cannonballed into the water.

"People feel good because they've gotten through half the course—and it's harder than they expected," the kid said. "Then they get to the Tower of Doom. Some cry."

"It's your turn," Z said, poking the boy's arm.

The kid laughed again and scrambled up to the board. "See ya tomorrow!" he shouted.

Z looked at Ava. "Go ahead."

Ava gripped the fat, metal rails and climbed the three steps. She licked her lips. She'd have to walk along the board, which stretched so far…and then there would be the fall—the jump. Her knees trembled. Blood rushed and roared in her ears.

"Come on!"

She turned. A teenage boy frowned. Two cool-looking girls about Ava and Z's age rolled their eyes so hard, they should have popped out.

"It's okay," Z said. "Just jump."

Ava took a deep breath. Bit her lip. She could do this. She could. As if someone else controlled her body, she took a step. The diving board felt like sandpaper.

"Go, Ava!" Z shouted. "Yay!"

Ava walked along the board—it was fine. Then the handrails ended. There was still a lot of board left with only air beside her. What if she fell over? She might hit her head.

"You got this," Z shouted.

Ava took a shaky step. She felt dizzy.

Suddenly, she wasn't at the pool. She lay in itchy grass with Mrs. Roberts, the mean school nurse, looming over her, yelling, "Calm down!" Her scowling face and the frizzy rainbow wig were such an odd combination, Ava almost wanted to laugh.

But she couldn't breathe.

Field Day had started out fun. At the dunk tank, Ava had hit the target on her first throw, sending the principal into the water to the cheers of her friends. Her egg-on-a-spoon relay team had come in third. She'd done well at the Hula-Hoop and limbo stations. She and Kylie had run the three-legged race and were laughing about it with Emma when Ava's heart jitter-juddered.

A fiery explosion erupted inside her, followed by crushing pain in her chest and stomach. Her lungs filled with cotton. She began to shake and sweat. She gasped for air. A terrible sense of doom—a darkness worse than any she'd known or imagined—choked her.

Mrs. Roberts shooed everyone away. "You're okay," she told Ava. She sounded mad. Her dry, powdery face, whiter than usual, pinched in disapproval. "Just breathe."

But Ava couldn't, and she couldn't explain why not. That made Mrs. Roberts madder.

Ava was dying. For-real, no-joke dying.

And she was alone.

Sirens screamed in the distance. Soon, an ambulance arrived, its lights flashing. Mrs. Roberts vanished, and a bald Black man with a kind face knelt beside her. His eyes met hers. "Hi, Ava. I'm Doug." He held a paper with her school picture and other information on it.

"I know you feel awful and it's very scary, but you're going to be okay." His voice was gentle but confident. "I'm going to put this on your finger—okay, Ava?—to check the oxygen in your blood. It won't hurt. We're going to take very good care of you and help you feel better."

Unlike Mrs. Roberts, who'd acted like Ava was throwing a tantrum to ruin Field Day, Doug understood what was happening to her, knew it was bad, and wanted to help. The EMTs carried Ava on a stretcher to the ambulance. They didn't use sirens or lights. Doug held Ava's hand the whole way, and together they practiced sniffing a rose and blowing out birthday candles.

Ava felt much better when they arrived at the emergency room. Dad, looking pale and scared, waited outside. He shook when he hugged her.

"Ava," he called now. "You don't have to jump."

His voice brought Ava back to Colorado. Back to the diving board. She took a breath and a step. Even though the railing had stopped, she could do this. She took a step and another.

With a shout, someone leaped from the super high dive and splashed Ava.

Her heart sped up. She couldn't walk on this shaky board without the rails, not with people jumping beside her, drenching her. Not with everyone staring and thinking she was a baby or a weirdo. They breathed without thinking about it. They couldn't imagine what it was like to be tricked by your own body, to be trapped, to be alone, smothered and helpless.

Ava crouched and gripped the board. Now she was in a horrible, awkward position—kind of in a ball. Slowly, she extended one leg back and then the other. In this position, Ava was more stable—but a zintebillion times more embarrassed. Plus: The board poked her palms and knees. Ava edged herself around—so very awkwardly, so very slowly—until she faced Z, the cool girls, and the rest of the line, which had grown. Plus: the lifeguard. Double plus: Dad.

Like the scaredy-cat, no-fun, thirty-year-old baby she was, Ava crawled to the ladder.

"Ava!" Dad raced up the diving board stairs.

The board rocked, and Ava ducked, gripped the edges harder, and whimpered.

The lifeguard's whistle shrieked.

"Sir! Get down!" Dad didn't move until the lifeguard yelled again. "Let me do my job!"

"What's happening?" a girl asked her father. Because: A crowd had gathered. Naturally.

"She's scared," the dad said. "They're helping her, see?"

"I'm brave," the little girl said.

Clutching the sides of the board, Ava wished she could make them all vanish. Make this—this Colorado everything—disappear.

"Hang on," the lifeguard said, and the board jolted again as she crept toward Ava. "Can you take my hand?"

The lifeguard looked strong and trustworthy. "Can you stand?" she asked.

Squeezing the lifeguard's hand, Ava dragged one foot forward until it was flat against the board, her opposite knee bent in a deep lunge.

"Good," the lifeguard said. "Now the other one?"

Pushing the board with her free hand for balance, Ava dragged her other foot forward.

"I've got you," the lifeguard said, and Ava rose on jelly legs.

The lifeguard tiny-stepped Ava off the board and down the ladder. The crowd cheered.

"Ava! Are you okay?" Dad tried to hug her, but Ava pushed away.

Her head buzzed. Her mouth was dry.

"That girl belongs in the baby pool," one of the cool girls sniffed. She sounded far away.

"No, she doesn't," another far-away girl said in Z's voice.

It wasn't only Z's voice. It was Z herself, defending Ava. "She's a scaredy-cat is all," Z continued. She didn't sound unkind, more like she was stating a fact.

CHAPTER 23

Ava ignored Dad and Z calling her name and left the pool without stopping for her towel or shoes. She ran to the one place Dad couldn't go—the women's bathhouse. Tears blurred her vision as Ava threaded around women and girls at the sinks and padded down the row of stalls to the last one. She slammed the door, shaking the metal walls.

Ava was mad at Z for follow-the-leader, for thinking Ava was no fun, for calling her a scaredy-cat; mad at the pool for having dangerous diving boards; mad at the lifeguard for rescuing her; mad at the cool girls for laughing. Ava was mad at Colorado for being so dangerous and Colorado-y; mad at Dad for embarrassing her and forcing her to go to Colorado, to go to the mountains, and to do the Mud Run; super mad at Dad for (maybe) having a baby with his Colorado girlfriend and (maybe) even getting married.

Mostly, Ava was mad, mad, mad at herself. Everyone else had jumped, even little kids. Why couldn't she?

The bathhouse door banged against the wall, and Ava held her breath. Banging doors was a Z thing. Ava considered standing on the toilet seat to hide, but that was dangerous. She could break an ankle. Hit her head.

"Ava?"

It was The Girlfriend. Ava squinted through the cracks in the doorframe. She stood outside her stall. "Are you okay?"

No. Ava was not. She was, after all, in Colorado.

"I see your feet, sweet pickle."

Sweet pickle.

A tear trickled down Ava's cheek.

"Can you please come out?"

Ava didn't want to. But she couldn't hide forever. With a shaky breath, she slid open the lock and slunk out of the stall—into The Girlfriend's open arms. Ava shut her eyes, sank into the hug, and inhaled the comforting, spicy-sweet scent.

Women and girls ducked in and out of stalls, talking, laughing, flushing, banging doors. They probably saw Ava crying, but for once she didn't care. Even if she had, she couldn't have stopped. Something inside her had cracked.

"Oh, sweet pickle," The Girlfriend said, rubbing her back. "It's okay."

Ava pulled back. "What's wrong with me?" Fresh tears made The Girlfriend's face blurry.

"Nothing!" The Girlfriend squeezed Ava's hand. "You're perfect."

Ava shook her head no and sniffed—a long, wet, gross sound. A perfect girl would have politely blown her nose on a tissue. A perfect girl wouldn't have ended up on her hands and knees on the diving board. A perfect girl wouldn't have had to be rescued. A perfect girl wouldn't have been a scaredy-cat, no-fun baby. Ava definitely wasn't perfect. Her eyes dropped to her bare feet on the germy tile.

"I have anxiety," she whispered. "It's new."

No, that wasn't right. Ava couldn't remember a time when she hadn't felt anxious. As she'd grown, she'd even worried about having so many worries. "I mean—" Ava looked up, into The Girlfriend's kind eyes. "I just found out. From a doctor."

"I'm glad you're getting help." The Girlfriend squeezed Ava's hand again. "But that doesn't mean you're not perfect, Ava."

That made no sense.

"You're perfectly human," The Girlfriend continued. "Everyone has challenges. It doesn't mean something's wrong with you. You were brave to try the diving board."

"But I didn't—"

The Girlfriend waved a hand. "I'm proud of you."

"But I—"

"You gave it your best shot, didn't you?"

It was true. Ava had been brave—at least until the railing ended.

"Maybe you'll jump next time?"

There would be no next time. Absolutely, positively not. Still, The Girlfriend had given Ava a lot to think about. "You said… nothing's wrong with me, even though I have anxiety?"

"Yes."

"Excuse us." A mom smiled as she herded three little kids past Ava and The Girlfriend and into the last stall.

This wasn't the best place for an important talk.

Even so, the wisp of an idea rose inside Ava. Like a fragile seedling breaking through the dark Iowa soil. She looked at The Girlfriend. "What did you say before? I'm perfect-something?"

"Perfectly human." The Girlfriend smiled again.

Yes, Ava had freaked out on the diving board, and it had been unbelievably embarrassing, and she couldn't imagine facing Z or Dad again. But what if, maybe, there wasn't anything wrong with her? The seedling of the idea grew like a baby plant, opening its tiny leaves and reaching to hug the sun: Ava wasn't the problem.

Colorado was the problem. Z was the problem. Dad was the problem.

Ava would show them. She would be brave at the Mud Run tomorrow—even at the Tower of Doom. She would beat Z and Dad.

No, she would crush them, destroy them.

She would prove there wasn't anything wrong with her.

But she couldn't do it alone. She'd need her partner.

The Girlfriend.

Jenn.

It was dark, and Z and Dad were asleep when Ava and Jenn slipped away early the next morning. Jenn wanted to visit her friend, Ruthie, a retired drama teacher who lived nearby and had a stash of costumes. It had been love at first sight when Jenn discovered the Big Bad Wolf costume. Ava was pretty sure the fake fur jumpsuit was a big, bad idea.

"Sometimes you have to sacrifice for fashion," Jenn said.

They also took a red cape, the only part of the Little Red Riding Hood outfit Ava felt okay wearing. (Especially after Ruthie mentioned "generations of sweaty teenagers" who'd worn the costumes.) After that, Ava and Jenn detoured to a discount store, where Jenn bought running tights, shorts, and a tank top—all red—to complete Ava's look.

Instead of heading back down to the resort when they'd finished, though, Jenn had turned the other way. "There's something I want you to see," she'd said. "It won't take long, and we're so close, I can't resist."

Now, she glanced at Ava as she drove. "We're almost there," Jenn said. "You okay?"

The narrow roads shot into the sky and whipped around the mountain at the last second, making Ava dizzy. Plus: Her stomach was Mud Run day jumpy. The boy at the pool had said people cried when they saw the Tower of Doom. (That night, Z had admitted she'd never heard of it.) And, although Ava had tried to put yesterday's diving board nightmare out of her mind, it lingered like a gloomy fog. But she didn't have the car throw-up feeling.

"Yeah. I'm okay."

They'd drained their water bottles and forgotten to refill them at Ruthie's. Jenn's cell phone had no signal. This high up, the air had zero oxygen, probably. There was nothing around, unless you counted wild animals on the prowl. Plus: plague-infected ground squirrels.

"This might be Monkey Mind, Ms. Ava." The voice was José's, inside Ava's head. Were a bunch of monkeys chasing each other in her brain and making her peek to see if the Jeep had enough gas? Ava breathed deeply and told her head monkeys to knock it off.

A few miles later, a sign announced a scenic lookout, and Jenn wheeled into an empty parking lot. She reached into the back seat, grabbed two winter jackets, and tossed one to Ava.

As Ava leaped from the Jeep, the sharp wind slapped her face, sliced through her jacket, and turned her bare legs to popsicles. Jenn grabbed Ava's hand and, together, they ran to the lookout area, shrieking at their shared, bone-chilling misery. "This is the tundra," Jenn shouted over the wild wind, which whipped her hair. "We're above the timberline."

The landscape was almost moonlike, with rocky peaks and dark valleys. The sun had nearly cleared the tallest spire, spilling a fiery glow. The mountains looked naked, stripped of their evergreens and hardwoods, their plants and people—their life. Even though it was June, icy snow trimmed rough crags.

But crumbly-looking lichen splayed across the rocks, and there were plants too, almost hiding: mossy clumps low to the ground and even flowers, defiant teeny blooms rising between sharp-toothed rocks.

The vast, stark terrain made Ava feel small, but in a good way. Like a God wink. She and Jenn stood there only a couple of minutes, but their teeth chattered as they dashed back to the Jeep. Jenn blasted the heater as she pulled onto the highway.

"I can't believe it's so cold," Ava said.

Maybe she'd never fly in space like Z someday, but she'd gone high into the Colorado mountains, so high even trees couldn't survive. Plus: She hadn't felt afraid. Only awed.

"Jenn? Thanks for taking me."

"You're welcome. I don't think your dad has ever been up there."

"How do those flowers survive?" Ava asked.

"It's amazing, isn't it? Those plants have found a way to live in one of the most extreme climates on Earth."

"But how?"

"They've created new ways to store food and water."

"You mean, the plants physically changed themselves?"

"Kind of freaky, isn't it?" Jenn said with a laugh. "It's a long, slow process, but they've adapted to their environment. And environments change too. Like, the mountains? They look so solid, but they're changing too. Everything is always changing."

Ava's hometown and the surrounding area had always seemed so fixed and constant. But now that she thought about it, it was changing too. Ms. Weber, the town librarian, had recently had a baby. The junior/senior high school was improving the gym. Even farmers planted different crops to help care for the land.

Maybe Ava was changing too? She hadn't wanted to do the Mud Run—no way, no how—but now she was…excited, maybe? Eager to beat Dad and Z for sure.

CHAPTER 24

Waiting near the lodge for Jenn to check them in for the Mud Run, Ava twirled and spun with her new cape. She pulled one side across her body, ducked her head, and became a vampire. She held the sides, raised her arms, and became a butterfly with massive red wings. Her magic cape would help her crush Dad and Z.

When the Big Bad Wolf finally lumbered down the lodge steps, she was with Dad and Z, who wore matching pink ballerina tutus over their shorts. "We're official!" Jenn waved two thin, plastic-y sheets with black numbers. She fastened each corner of Ava's race bib to her tank top with safety pins.

"Hey," Dad said, "look at you."

"Look at you, back," Ava said.

"I like it." He twisted, making his tutu flutter.

While Dad was excited about his costume, Z seemed...the opposite. Her Z sparkle had dulled. Her eyes were puffy and rimmed with dark circles. Her face, usually animated with an impish expression—tilted head, single quirked eyebrow, lopsided grin—sagged. Even her tutu drooped. Z—almost always dancing, skipping, wiggling, climbing, chattering—stood still and quiet.

Ava had expected her to be mad about not racing with Rodrigo. Her sorrow was worse. She touched Z's arm. "It'll be okay," she whispered.

Z turned away.

They walked to the course in silence, joining a parade of princesses, pirates, zombies, ninjas, dinosaurs, superheroes, Star Wars characters, and even Santa and an elf. A balloon canopy stretched over the starting line, and orange cones marked the racecourse. Another space was roped off for people to watch.

Ava's mouth went dry. Her hand jumped to her watch—but, of course, her wrist was bare. She'd stored it in her clean-clothes bag. It felt as if part of herself were missing.

She'd been so excited. Now, she was scared. She stood on tiptoe, trying to find some of the obstacles. She couldn't see them. But there was José, talking to two young women, all wearing referee shirts and whistles around their necks. Ava dashed over to them.

"Looking good, Iowa Girl," José said, smacking her palm.

"Are you a ref?" Ava cringed at her obvious question. "I mean, are there rules and stuff?"

José shook his head. "We're here to help everything run smoothly. You ready to race?"

"Is it true?" Ava swallowed. "There's a Tower of Doom? Kids cry—"

"Ah, Li'l A. That's what they want you to think. Part of the thrill." He grinned down at her. "If it really were dangerous, you'd see all these hurt people stumbling around, moaning and bleeding all over the place as they went through the course. There'd be all these lawsuits. You think they'd put up with that year after year?"

That made sense.

"They don't want to make you miserable," José said. "They want you to have fun."

Colorado people definitely had a different concept of fun than regular people in Iowa. The whole idea of running in the mountains with no oxygen was ridiculous enough without throwing in mud, water, and super-high towers.

He lowered his voice. "Ropes stretched over a frame, that's the so-called Tower of Doom. You've got to hold on and climb it like a wobbly ladder, Li'l A, one step at a time."

"But it's super tall?"

He shrugged. "A few more steps. You got that." José bent down and met her eyes. "I'm going to tell you something I didn't learn until college, but I think you're mature enough to handle it, okay?"

Excited, Ava scooted closer.

"You've got to learn the difference between what's possible and probable. You feel me? Don't make a mountain out of a molehill."

The expression meant taking something small—like a stubbed toe—and acting like it was a super-big deal, like a broken leg. But how did it work when you really were in the mountains?

"What I'm saying is don't make situations worse in your head than they are in real life."

Had she done that? Did the monkeys have something to do with it?

"All ten- through twelve-year-olds report to the starting line," someone said over a loudspeaker. "Bring your adult. Spectators, please stay behind the ropes."

"I've got to go. Thanks for your help!" Ava hurried back to her group, her mind jumping from molehills to mountains, from possibles to probables.

Possible: A thing *could* happen.

Probable: A thing was *likely* to happen.

Example: Falling from the tower.

Possible? No doubt.

Probable? Maybe…not?

Ava felt like she was on the verge of solving an impossible math problem. What if the Tower of Doom wasn't a mountain? What if it were a molehill?

After Field Day, some people said Ava had overexerted herself in the three-legged race. But she'd never had trouble in PE and her health was excellent. Dr. C. didn't think anything at Field Day had caused Ava's panic attack. Unfortunately, she said, panic attacks could happen at any time for any reason. Or for no reason. They were awful, Dr. C said, but they could not kill her, even though it felt that way. The horrible feelings would pass.

If running around at Field Day hadn't caused her panic attack, maybe Ava didn't have to be so afraid of the Mud Run? What if the Mud Run was a molehill too? As Ava breathed deeply, a truly shocking thought arrived:

What if the mountains…

what if all of Colorado…

were molehills?

"Ava!" Dad didn't look happy. "Where were you?"

"Just over there." She pointed. "Talking to a friend." Warmth spread across her cheeks.

"I can't believe you'd run off like that," Dad said, "especially in a crowd."

It was kind of funny. It was almost the same thing Jenn had said to Z at the airport.

They headed toward the starting line, but it was less line and more human blob. Ava did a double take. Was that…? His back faced her, but the hair…and he was looking for someone. "Z!" Ava shouted. "Look!"

"Daddy," Z shrieked.

Rodrigo turned, his grin lopsided. The crowd parted as he strutted toward them.

Z threw herself at him.

"Heard you needed a partner," Rodrigo said with a laugh.

"Eric, this is Rodrigo." Jenn looked coolly at her ex-husband. "This is Eric."

"Nice to meet you." Dad extended his hand, and Rodrigo tapped it with his fist.

"He's Z's partner," Jenn said.

Dad glanced from Jenn to Z, who was hanging on Rodrigo's arm. "It's okay if you want to do it with your dad."

"Yay!" Z's tutu bounced as she jumped.

Ava wasn't sure, but she thought she saw a flicker of disappointment behind Dad's eyes. He patted Ava's back. "It's fine."

Except it wasn't. Ava couldn't demolish him if Dad didn't compete.

"Hey, Ava," Rodrigo said. "Qué pasa, chica?" *What's up, girl?*

"Buenos días!" *Good morning.* Ava turned to Dad. "We always speak Spanish together."

"Oh." Dad fidgeted with the number pinned to his chest. "That's fun."

He sounded almost sad, though.

"Hey, man," Rodrigo said to Dad. "What's your shoe size?"

"Last call to the starting line, racers," the loudspeaker said.

"These are custom," Rodrigo said. "Alligator."

Everyone stared at his boots. But it was obvious Rodrigo's shoes weren't the only problem. He wore fancy jeans and a white button-down shirt. White!

Dad looked at his beat-up tennis shoes. "They're elevens. Canvas."

He kicked off his shoes and unpinned his race bib. He started to remove the tutu, but Rodrigo waved. "I'm good. Keep the glasses too."

Rodrigo was too cool to wear taped-up glasses, even when he thought they were part of a costume. But Dad, who'd had to wear them for most of their trip, hadn't complained once, even though it wasn't his fault they were broken. It was as if the gentlest breeze had kissed a dying ember. A fire woke inside Ava, roaring to life, its flames kicking high and hot, like a dangerous Colorado wildfire. That's who she would be—Colorado Wildfire Girl. Z had dumped Dad. Ava was going to scorch Z and Rodrigo.

Jenn bent down to Ava. "Shoes double-tied?" she whispered. "Laces pushed inside?"

"Yes and yes."

Jenn pulled on her fuzzy wolf's cap and tied the strings under her chin. With a steely side glance at Rodrigo, she said, "Let's do this."

―――――――――――

The first obstacle rose in the distance, a hay bale tower surrounded by dirty water. Ava sailed up and over the haystack, as she'd done a centrillion times in her grandparents' barn.

"Go, Baby Ava Girl," Dad shouted from the viewing area. "Come on, Jenn!"

Ava felt good as they ran to the next station. Racers had to army crawl—drag themselves with their forearms—through muddy trenches under low nets. Because of her size, Ava wondered if she could regular-crawl?

When it was her turn, Ava ripped through the trench on her hands and knees like a scuttling mud insect. She was sweating and breathing hard when she finished, but she'd made great time. As she waited for Jenn, Ava searched for Z and Rodrigo.

"Great job," Jenn said, breathless and mud-caked. "Do you need a break?"

"No. Do you?"

"Let's go."

Several feet ahead, the sun glinted off a large, rectangular pit filled with water. The third obstacle. Several racers were splashing through the water.

"Wait." Ava slowed. Two teams passed and jumped into the water with victory shouts. "They're going to get stuck," Ava said. "You have to ease in, and lift with your toes when you walk, so you don't lose your shoes."

Jenn shook her head. "How do you know that?"

Ava grinned. "Grandmom's pond."

She and Jenn were the only racers who sat on the pit's edge and slipped into the sun-warmed water. It whooshed into Ava's shoes, and her shorts ballooned. Her feet sunk into ooze. The water reached Jenn's hips and Ava's chest. Holding hands, they stepped tentatively.

"Nice and slow," Jenn said.

It was exactly like Grandmom's pond.

Except: Creepy crawlies in Colorado water could make people really sick. If those tiny parasites got into her…

No. Ava wasn't going to think about that—and she wasn't going to think *like* that, either. Because: Getting sick from dirty water drops might be possible—some had splashed her face—but it wasn't probable. Ava clutched that idea like a life jacket. She imagined herself in Grandmom's pond, Mouse happily dog-paddling beside her.

Two arguing princesses fell over with a shriek, still clutching each other. Ava and Jenn shared a secret smile. It was cool how going slowly made you fast sometimes.

After crossing the pit, they crawled onto the spongy ground. Jenn rested on her side.

Ava crouched beside her. "Are you okay?"

"Mmm-hmm." Jenn didn't move as racers scrabbled out near her and stumbled onward.

"Do you need a drink? The medical tent's right over there."

"I'm fine." Jenn pushed onto her hands and knees. It was as if an ancient creature was leaving her slime home for the first time, having grown fur legs.

Jenn plodded to the next obstacle as if wearing ankle weights. Dirty water poured off her.

"I can't remember," Ava said, trying to keep her face serious, "when does this get fun?"

Jenn laughed. "Oh, Ava," she said, pulling her into a hug. "I love you."

As far as hugs go, it was dirty, soggy, and stinky. But Ava wished Jenn's wet fur-arms had held on a bit longer.

"Oh, I'm sorry." The twinkle had returned to Jenn's eyes. "Did I get you wet?"

Ava answered with a gentle shove.

"When does this get fun?" Jenn mimicked, then laughed again.

A distinctive voice cut through the cheering, shouting, sloshing, thudding, grunting, and splashing around them. "My foot! Help! Rodrigo!"

In the distance, Z crouched near the top of a very tall cargo net stretched across a frame.

Ava and Jenn ran.

CHAPTER 25

Ava threw herself at the Tower of Doom like a hyper kitten. It was like scaling a twisty-bendy, ever-changing, un-sturdy rope ladder. It shifted with the racers' movements, and Ava had to hold tight. The safety mats below didn't look soft.

She'd never climbed so high. One step at a time. That's what José had said.

One.

One.

One.

Ava neared the top. She didn't look down. It would freak her mind monkeys.

Z's kicking roiled the net. Jenn, surprisingly, had made little progress up the structure.

Ava pulled a shaky leg over the top of the frame. She could do this. Slowly, she swung the other leg over. Exhaled. She'd gotten herself up and over, apparently, without Z seeing. Like a fly trapped in a web, she hadn't moved. Where was Rodrigo?

Ava shut her eyes, letting the net carry her like waves.

She wanted to beat Z.

But she couldn't leave her.

She had to beat Z.

But Z was stuck.

Ava opened her eyes and twisted around, searching for Dad. It was Rodrigo who drew her eyes. His shirt was filthy. His soaked, trendy jeans fought his wide belt, trying to fall down. He wore only one of Dad's shoes. Did he know Z was in trouble? Was he taking a break? Or…selfies? He posed with fans, laughing, signing autographs, giving hugs.

A chill swept over Ava.

Right behind it, fire.

Because: Z wanted so badly to spend time with Rodrigo and compete in the Mud Run with him. Plus: She needed him, and he was more interested in his fans than his own daughter.

Dad had plenty of faults. But he was there for her. Always, always. And Ava was lucky to have him. The thought—the pure, electric truth of it—struck her like lightning.

Ava raised a wobbly leg and angled down the other side of the Tower of Doom. "Excuse me," she said, moving against the tide of surprised and irritated racers. She sidestepped toward Z, avoiding elbows, knees, and feet that could crush fingers and knock her down.

"Hey." Ava touched Z's leg.

Z stared down. "I'm stuck!"

"Let me see." Ava picked at the netting. How had it wound around Z's foot? That is, she assumed Z's foot was somewhere in that disgusting mud ball. It was especially tricky because Ava had to keep one hand on the moving net.

"Hurry," Z yelled.

Ava scowled. "You're lucky I'm helping at all."

"Sorry. My hands really hurt."

With a silent groan and her stomach churning, Ava dug into the thick, squashy, dirty mud. She threw handfuls, trying not to hit anybody.

"Oops!" She'd nailed Jenn's fur chest. "Sorry! I'm trying to find the laces."

"I'm stuck," Z wailed. "My hands hurt a lot a lot."

"Where's Rodrigo?" Jenn looked around. "I don't believe this," she muttered as she and Ava excavated Z's wet, filthy shoelace. "No, I do. Rodrigo lives in Rodrigo World."

She swore, shocking a ninja, princess, and pirate climbing nearby.

With much of the mud cleared, Jenn and Ava loosened the netting around Z's tennis shoe.

"You're good," Ava hollered. She wiped her hand on her cape. "Hey," she said, turning back, "do you—"

Incredibly, Z was already at the top. Carefully gripping the frame, she flipped over, spraying dried mud and landing with her back against the other side of the net.

They had to catch up with her! "Come on," Ava said.

Jenn waved a grimy hand. "Go ahead." She sounded weary.

Ava hesitated. Racers jostled around them. "Are you okay?"

"Yeah." Jenn shut her eyes.

Ava's knuckles were white from gripping the rope. "But are you, really?"

"I'm…right behind…you."

But she didn't move. Jenn's breathing seemed heavier than usual. Was her color off? How white was "pale"? With all the dirt on Jenn's face, how could anyone tell? What if…?

Ava's knees turned to water. Jenn hadn't wanted to ride horses or do the zip line. She hadn't taken the allergy medicine. She'd been a little sick and a lot tired. She'd worn loose tops. What if…

Jenn opened her eyes and smiled weakly. "Go get our girl."

Ava took a breath and climbed the wiggly net. Again. What if those sticks in Jenn's bathroom had been from two months ago? What if she really were pregnant right now? When Ava arrived at the top—again—her heart sank. Z had vanished. Without even saying thanks.

As soon as her feet touched ground, she found Dad in the spectator area. "I'm so proud of you, Baby Ava Girl."

Jenn moved so slowly, Ava couldn't watch. A sloth could have beaten her to the top. What if she was dehydrated? Suffering altitude sickness? That could hurt Jenn but also her baby. If she were pregnant.

"She shouldn't be doing this," Ava said.

"Jenn's an athlete, Ava," Dad said. "She knows how to take care of herself."

Ava couldn't look into his kind eyes. Plus: his broken glasses.

She kicked an imaginary rock. "She shouldn't have worn that stupid costume."

Tell him. Tell him. *Tell him.*

The words stuck in her throat.

Ava turned and headed back toward Jenn.

"Don't worry," Dad called, super unhelpfully.

Jenn had made it over and down. Now she leaned against the edge of the tower, panting. Her eyes were closed again, her face red.

Tentatively, Ava stretched to untie the bow under Jenn's chin and peeled off the fur cap. Jenn's eyes fluttered open, then closed again. The cap was heavy, wet, and super gross. Even worse: Jenn's hair, pulled into a low pony, looked as if it had been doused with a bucket of water. Was that sweat? That couldn't be good.

"Breeze," Jenn whispered. Her voice sounded strange, and her eyes remained closed.

It didn't matter if you were an athlete or used to mountains. If you didn't drink enough water, you could get dehydrated. Wearing a fur jumpsuit, weighed down with mud and water, wouldn't help. Ava touched Jenn's filthy cheek. So hot! Was it heat exhaustion? That could turn into deadly heat stroke.

And what if she were pregnant?

A ref walked over. "You need to move out of the way," she said.

Ava touched Jenn's back. "Come on."

Jenn's eyes opened but didn't seem to focus. "We can't…go… back there."

"Where?" Ava asked, confused. She took Jenn's arm.

Jenn shook her off. "Stop fussing."

"We need to go over here," Ava said firmly, and Jenn followed her to the sidelines. "You need water." Ava crossed her arms and cocked her hip—imitating Z—so Jenn would know she was serious. It was obvious Jenn wasn't feeling well. She was usually so reasonable. Why was she fighting this?

Jenn's breathing sounded like Mouse on a hot day. "Have to… beat him."

Rodrigo. Jenn must really hate him if beating him in a stupid Mud Run meant that much.

"That doesn't matter," Ava said. "You need water. Seriously, Jenn."

"How much more?" Jenn asked.

"Huh?"

"This. Race." Jenn took a step and faltered. She might have fallen if Ava hadn't caught her arm. But Jenn didn't seem to care. "How many obstacles?"

"We're halfway," Ava said.

Jenn squinted into the distance. Maybe she hadn't heard?

"That was the fourth," Ava said. "There are eight, total."

"So, how many…"

That did it. If Jenn couldn't do simple mental math, something was wrong. Definitely, absolutely, for sure. Confusion was a sign of altitude sickness. That could kill her and her baby. If Jenn wouldn't get water for herself, maybe she would for Ava?

"I'm so thirsty." Ava wobbled her head, as if she might faint.

"Okay," Jenn said.

Maybe Ava was a good actor after all? They veered toward the first aid station, Jenn walking with her arms raised, fingers locked behind her head. She seemed to be moving better after her short rest. Everything was going to be okay.

"Superstar, going far," someone in the crowd shouted.

Jenn stopped, alert as Mouse sensing a nearby cat. (His cat prejudice was his only flaw.)

Rodrigo waited in line for the fifth obstacle.

Jenn charged at him like an angry rhino. "Where's your daughter?" she yelled.

Rodrigo grinned. "Finally catching up?"

"Your daughter was stuck. You were missing in action, like always."

"What's your problem?" Rodrigo raised his chin.

"You, Rodrigo Lopez—"

"What's going on?" Z strode toward them. She looked from one parent to the other.

"She's on my case," Rodrigo said with an exaggerated, bored shrug. "As per her usual."

"Jenn?" Ava whispered. She still held the wet wolf's cap. "We need to get water."

"Right." Jenn continued glaring at Rodrigo. "It's always about you, isn't it, superstar?"

Racers stared. Some from the crowd held up cell phones. Were they filming?

Rodrigo raised his hands. "What do you want from me?"

"Be a father," Jenn shouted. Except there was a swear too.

It was a relief to see Dad striding toward them, but only racers were allowed on the course. He touched Jenn's wet, dirty fur arm. "Is everything okay?"

"Hunky-dory, amigo," Rodrigo said.

"Are you okay?" Dad asked Jenn.

Look at her red face, Ava wanted to shout. Look how sweaty she is. Look how she's breathing. Did you see her almost fall? No, Ava wanted to scream and scream and scream, Jenn was not okay. If Jenn wasn't going to help herself—and the baby—Ava would have to help them.

CHAPTER 26

"Dad?" Ava tugged his shirt. "Jenn needs a doctor."

"I'm fine," Jenn said.

"Then why can't you do simple math?" Ava said.

Dad looked at Ava. "What are you talking about?"

"Why do you always have to be so mean to him?" Z said to her mother. She leaned into Rodrigo, who draped a dirty arm around her shoulder. "Why can't we be a normal family?"

"Mackenzie," Jenn said. "You need—"

"Why can't you ever, *ever* call me Z?"

"Come on, Z." Dad's voice was low and angry.

"Who are you again?" Rodrigo stepped toward Dad and puffed out his chest. Dad stayed put, even though Rodrigo was crowding his personal space. They eyed each other, backs straight, jaws tight. Ava held her breath. It was like they were having a monster staring contest, but it wasn't fun or funny. Ava was proud of Dad for remaining calm, but she wished he'd taken off his broken glasses and tutu.

"He's the man who's been here," Jenn said, stepping forward too, so that everybody was too close to everybody. "The man who was going to race with your daughter."

"Come on, Rodrigo," Z said. "We have a race to win."

Rodrigo stared at Dad a second longer, then tapped his fingers to his forehead, as if tipping an invisible hat—or saluting—and followed Z.

"Dad," Ava said, "Jenn might have altitude sickness—"

Dad sighed. "Will you please—*please*—stop worrying, Ava?" He sounded annoyed that Ava cared about his girlfriend.

Apparently Rodrigo wasn't finished. He strode back toward Jenn, hobbling in one shoe. "You're telling me to be a father?" he said, repeating Jenn's swear. "I *am* a father." He added a swear of his own.

Ava's stomach clenched. She wasn't finished, either. But what if she were wrong?

"Say what you want," Rodrigo continued, "about me—"

But what if she were right? The baby could be in danger too.

"She's pregnant," Ava said, waving at Jenn. "She needs water."

Rodrigo didn't even pause. "But don't you dare make Z think I don't love her. That—"

Had they even heard Ava? She had to speak up. "She's going to have a baby."

"I don't make her think that," Jenn shouted. "You do an awesome job all on your own."

Ava felt as invisible and silent as Pretend Mouse at her side.

Z had lingered a few feet away but returned now too. "Stop yelling at him," she yelled.

Ava really hoped she was right. She took a big breath. She needed to be loud, loud, *loud*. "She needs to go to first aid! She's not well, and she's pregnant!"

Jenn stepped back, almost as if her knees had buckled. Her eyes widened, and her hand flew to her furry throat.

"Who?" Z whirled around. "What?"

"Ava!" Dad frowned. "Why would you say such a thing?"

"Who's pregnant?" Z said.

"Don't look at me, kid." Rodrigo cocked a single eyebrow, like Z. "Does the Big Bad Wolf have a bun in the oven?"

"Shut up," Dad said.

Ava gasped. She'd never, ever heard him say those words—until they'd arrived in Colorado, where he'd said them three times.

"Ava," Dad said, "you owe Jenn an apology."

Their eyeballs burned into her.

Ava felt sick.

"No, she doesn't," Jenn whispered, taking Ava's hand. "We're going to medical."

As Dad hurried after them, Z's voice carried. "Is Mom going to have a baby?"

At the first aid station, paramedics whisked Jenn into a large tent. Dad paced nearby, his tutu bobbing. Ava wanted to talk to him, but what could she say? Plus: He looked mad.

She turned toward a folding table that held paper cups of water for the racers. She selected one and drank without pausing, refilled it from the spout of a large plastic cooler, and drained it again. Then, unsure what to do with herself, Ava filled more cups and lined them up, careful to keep her dirty fingers off the rims.

"Is this free?"

Two muddy girls, both dressed as Rey from Star Wars, stood at the table.

"Drink as much as you want," Ava said, glancing at Dad, who continued to pretend she didn't exist. "It's important to stay hydrated."

Z and Rodrigo arrived a couple of minutes later. As Z started toward the tent, Ava said, "The paramedic said to wait here."

Z glared and brushed past her, almost toppling the row of cups.

Rodrigo approached Dad and kicked off his single remaining tennis shoe. "The other one's still in that water pit. I couldn't get it. I'm sorry."

Dad nodded. He wore his normal tennis shoes from his clean-clothes bag. He retrieved Rodrigo's fancy boots and handed them to him.

"Thanks." Rodrigo eyed Dad. "So—" Rodrigo's mouth rose in a slow grin. "I hear your girlfriend's expecting."

When Dad didn't respond, Rodrigo raised a single eyebrow again. "Seems like little Ava is the only one who knows anything about it, though?"

Dad stepped toward Rodrigo. "We're not having this conversation."

"Okay, okay." Rodrigo raised his hands and stepped back. "I'm confused, though, because I heard you two might be on the outs."

"Where'd you hear that?"

"I don't reveal my sources," Rodrigo said.

Both men glanced at Ava, who gripped the table edge to keep from toppling over.

"We're not having this conversation," Dad repeated.

Rodrigo backed farther away, chuckling softly. He dropped to the ground. "Z?" he yelled as he picked dried mud from his feet. He had frog toes, long and bony. "Z! Come here!"

"How's your mom?" Dad asked as Z stepped out of the tent. "Is she okay?"

"I think so." Z sounded distracted. She hurried to Rodrigo.

"I've got to go, kiddo."

"We haven't finished the race!"

Dad went into the tent.

Ava wanted to hear Z and Rodrigo's conversation, but she didn't want to be obvious. She took her time filling and arranging more cups.

"You said you'd run it with me." Z dropped to the ground beside him.

Rodrigo fished his sock out of his boot. "We got waylaid, didn't we? I've got to go."

"Nooooo." Z practically cried the word.

Rodrigo grimaced and wiped a hand over his mouth. His eyes looked so sad for a moment. "Don't whine," he said, wiggling the sock onto his foot. "You know how it is."

"We're going to dinner!"

"Can't." Rodrigo tugged on his boots.

"But you said—"

"I didn't know I'd be covered in mud, Z."

Z's knee bounced, bounced, bounced. "Mud runs are muddy, Rodrigo."

"I didn't know about the Mud Run." He gestured at his wrecked jeans. "Obviously."

"You knew about it when you told me you couldn't do it."

Rodrigo sighed and shook his head. "I forgot it was today." He stood. "Come on, Mackenzie, don't be a brat."

Ava waited for Z to correct him about her name.

"You don't even know I haven't gotten my period yet," Z said.

"What?" Rodrigo unpinned his race bib and dropped it on the ground. (On top of everything else, he was a litter bug!) He extended a hand to Z. "Give Papi a muddy hug."

Z let him pull her to her feet. She stared at the ground.

"Come on," Rodrigo said. "I've got a big shoot tonight—with important people."

Ava sucked in a breath. Was he saying those people were more important than Z?

Rodrigo gave Z a quick kiss on the cheek. "Be good," he said. "And if you can't be good, you know what to do." He grinned.

"Be good-looking," she replied dully.

Rodrigo laughed. "That's it!" He didn't seem to notice or, maybe, care about, Z's glum tone. "Adios, mi amiga Ava!"

As he left, someone in the crowd shouted, "Superstar, going far!"

Z snatched Rodrigo's race bib from the ground and threw it in the trash next to the water table. Ava stood beside the table. Dad had returned from the tent and resumed pacing. They didn't look at each other. The shouts, laughter, and screeches of racers amplified their silence.

A few minutes later, Jenn joined them, wearing the tank top and shorts she'd had on under her wolf costume.

"Are you okay?" Ava asked.

"A little overheated, but I'm fine."

Z pushed past Ava to get to her mom. "Are you really pregnant?"

"I was going to tell you." Jenn's eyes flickered to Dad. "I was waiting for the right time."

Z stabbed an accusing finger at Dad. "Is he the father?"

Jenn pressed a dirty hand to her forehead and shut her eyes for a moment. "Eric and I need to talk—in private."

"Wait!" Z grabbed her mom's arm. "Are you and Rodrigo getting back together?"

"What? No." Jenn frowned. "Why would you think that?" She glanced at the people milling around and potentially eavesdropping. "Let's get out of here."

"But is Eric the father?" Z insisted. "Why won't you answer?"

Dad's face was red.

"Of course he is," Jenn said.

"What?" Ava said, striding toward Dad. "No. *No.*" Of course, he'd been the likeliest suspect. But Ava had so hoped it wasn't true. "You said you weren't even talking about babies!"

"They must have done more than talk." Z raised a single eyebrow like her dad.

Ava whirled around to face Z. "Everything's a big joke to you, isn't it?"

That, apparently, was the cue for everyone to talk at once.

"Stop," Jenn shouted, raising her hands. "We need to talk, and we will." She plucked at her filthy shorts. "But I need a shower first."

They didn't talk as they retraced the race route back to the start, Dad carrying Jenn's costume as if it were a wounded dog. They didn't talk when they added their old, muddy shoes to the recycle pile. They didn't talk when they trudged all the way back to the main lodge for their clean-clothes bags. When Jenn saw the shower line stretching around the women's bathhouse, she said one word: a swear.

They took their places in line, and Dad waited with them. For once, Dad and Jenn didn't talk nonstop. They weren't talking at all. Z paced, adjusted her ponytail, rocked back and forth, rose up and down on her toes, swung her arms, and squeezed her hands into fists. She paced away from the line, then suddenly strode back toward Jenn. "Why didn't you tell us?" she said, crossing her arms. "It's a very big deal."

"I'm sorry." Jenn reached for Z, but she scooted away. "This vacation was supposed to be about the four of us. I didn't…" Jenn's voice trailed off.

"But why…*why* would you tell her"—Z gestured wildly at Ava—"and not—" Her voice cracked, and she pressed her hands to the sides of her head, as if trying to keep her brain inside.

"Oh, honey." Jenn rushed to Z but stopped short of hugging her. "I didn't tell anyone."

Dad's jaw tensed. "What happened, Ava? How did you know?"

Three sets of eyes drilled into her. The two women in line ahead of them seemed to lean back, as if they, too, were curious.

Ava's fingers went to her watch. It wasn't there. Only mud. They wouldn't understand how exciting it had been to touch and smell and try Jenn's hair product. Grandmom and Mrs. Mendez didn't have things like that. Dad didn't even use conditioner.

Ava looked at Jenn. "I tried your hair stuff. I—I'm sorry." She took a breath, her heart beating too fast. "I made a mess. By accident. There was water everywhere." Ava remembered her panic. "I got a towel and…I—I found the sticks."

"Sticks?" Dad said.

"Pregnancy tests," Jenn said. "I saved them…to show you."

CHAPTER 27

"There's mud in my underwear," Z wailed from the neighboring shower stall.

"It's everywhere." Gingerly, Ava peeled off each mud-soaked part of her costume. "It's…"

"Oh," said Jenn, in a stall across from them. "This is bad."

"Disgusting," Ava said.

"How did it get in my underwear, though?" Z yelled.

"I'm going to throw up," Ava said.

"You better give me more warning this time," Z said. "That was so disgusting in the car."

"Z, please," Jenn said.

Hope flickered in Ava. Maybe—*maybe*—Jenn didn't hate her?

After showering, they met Dad on the lodge's front porch. "Sunscreen?" he asked Ava, as if he had to pay a millibitrillion dollars for each word he spoke to her.

She nodded.

They stowed the garbage bag with their muddy clothes in the Jeep's trunk. Then they started up the trail toward the hermitage.

Ava quickened her pace to match Jenn's. "I thought you were in trouble. That's why—"

"I know—"

"You didn't look right, and—"

"The paramedic said she was fine." Dad's tone left no doubt he was mad at Ava.

But all she'd done was be concerned about Jenn and her baby. Her and Dad's baby.

The thought made her dizzy.

The trees seemed to have closed in on the narrow trail, cloaking it in shadow. The wind had grown even stronger. A fat raindrop splashed on Ava's arm. Another hit her cheek.

She was weary from rising early, competing in half of the Mud Run, and spilling Jenn's secret to the whole world. But Ava ran. No way was she getting caught outside in a Colorado thunderstorm. Especially on a mountain.

She almost beat Z.

Soon after they arrived at the hermitage, the sky burst like a water balloon on a driveway. The forest and mountains blurred through the windows, as if the little cabin were crying.

Z dropped onto the bed. "What's going to happen?" she asked.

Jenn sat beside her and motioned for Ava to join them. "You're going to be big sisters." She smiled at each of them.

Hearing it out loud sparked through Ava. She'd always wanted a sister—but, really, any sibling would be nice. But if the baby lived in Denver, they wouldn't know each other.

"Are you getting married?" Z asked.

It was thrilling how that girl could say anything and everything, whenever she wanted.

"Eric and I have a lot to discuss," Jenn said, glancing at him. "This is new for him too."

Z tugged her mother's arm. "But are you?"

This might have been an excellent time for Dad to fall to one knee, pledge his undying love, and propose. But he stood by the desk, a red-faced, scowling statue.

Ava jumped up and stalked over to him. "Do you love her or not?" she demanded.

"Of course." Dad frowned at Ava, but as he glanced at Jenn, his expression softened.

This made Ava angrier. Why hadn't he told her the truth about how he felt?

"I'm sorry this has been so confusing," Jenn said. She looked at Dad. "Can we talk in the tent?"

Wait, what? Ava looked around. That was it? There were still so many things she needed to know—and, suddenly, surprisingly, so many things she needed to say too.

The truth about their cabin reservation, for starters.

Because: Jenn really was pregnant. Dad really was the father.

Despite all her worrying and plotting, Ava hadn't really, truly, deep-down believed it.

But it was true. It was serious. And it involved a whole future person. Ava had to come clean and stop her plan before it was too late.

They'd be mad. Hurt too. Maybe they'd hate her, even Dad.

It was possible.

Was it probable?

What if Jenn didn't want Z or her baby to spend time with someone as awful as Ava? What if Jenn didn't want to either?

Ava shouldn't say anything.

Except…

She kept thinking about Kylie saying she was a good person and about what José had said that first day, how everything was connected. Ava had had plenty of reasons for what she'd done. Good reasons. Still, she'd hurt Z, Jenn, and Dad. On purpose.

She didn't have to tell them. They thought the resort had made a mistake. Dad had even stopped asking about the glitter. Besides, with Jenn's pregnancy confirmed, this wasn't the time to talk about the bad things Ava had done.

Except…

If she didn't tell them, her betrayal would linger like a physical thing between them. Ava knew this absolutely, even though she wasn't sure how she knew it. Dad, Jenn, and Z deserved to know that Ava was the reason they'd had a bad time and were cranky with each other. She needed to confess and apologize to all of them, to try to heal the hurt she'd caused, even though Jenn and Dad were already at the door. Even though they needed to go to the tent and talk about their baby.

"Uh," Ava said, her heart racing. "I kind of need to tell you a thing."

Z jumped up. "You snooped in my stuff too, didn't you?"

"No!" Ava wrapped her arms around her middle and watched the floor like it was her favorite TV show. "It's, uh…it's bad."

"What is it? Did something happen?" Dad crossed the room. "You need to tell us, Ava." He put a hand on her shoulder. "Look at me."

Dad looked scared, as if he feared something bad had happened *to* her.

"Whatever it is," he whispered, "it'll be okay. But you need to tell us, all right?"

This was awful, familiar territory: someone insisting that Ava talk, with predictable results—her throat frozen and unable to form words even though she wanted to. But it had never happened with Dad.

Ava shook her head no.

"Yes." He thought she was refusing to speak, not that she couldn't. "Tell us."

"It's better to get it over with," Z said.

They surrounded her, standing too close. Inconceivably and apparently without anyone else noticing, the small cabin's wooden walls had moved closer, boxing them in, tighter and tighter, taking most of the oxygen when the stupid mountain air already didn't have enough.

Ava gulped.

Inside her head, she named five things she could see: Bed. Allergy medicine. Jenn. Z. Dad.

This was a mistake. She didn't have to tell.

Four things she could feel: The floor supporting her. Dad's hand. The glass face of her watch. Z's burning stare.

There wasn't anything Ava could do now about the bad things she'd done before.

Three sounds: Rain on the roof and windows. The squeaky floor under Z's shifting feet. Ava's shaky breath, in and out.

Two smells: Christmas trees and sunscreen.

Did they really need to know? What if, from now on, Ava was good?

One good thing about herself.

Ava felt guilty and ashamed. She'd been mean. But that wasn't all she was.

One good thing about herself: Ava told the truth.

Almost always.

She knew what she needed to do. But she was so scared. Maybe she could call on Pretend Mouse for help? Maybe she could be like an actor in a play, reciting words from a script? She inhaled and noticed her shoulders up by her ears. She exhaled, let them drop.

"I canceled our cabin," Ava whispered. "It was me."

Z's arm shot out and grabbed Ava's. "What do you mean?"

"Let go." Jenn pulled Z to her. "Give her space."

Z's eyes widened. "The resort didn't make a mistake. We've been staying *here*"—she motioned around the small room—"without electricity, without running water—"

"No, hold on." Dad raised a hand. "We're misunderstanding. What happened, Ava?" His other hand gently squeezed her shoulder, as if he could press a different truth from her.

But Z continued fitting the pieces together. "You didn't want to come to the mountains." She broke away from her mother and strode toward Ava. "You sabotaged us. You thought the lodge would send us home!"

"Inside voice," Jenn said.

"Ava?" Dad looked so sad and confused. "That's not true, is it?"

"Yes," Ava croaked. "It's true."

"Do you know how much that cabin cost?" Dad said.

Ava swallowed. "And I—I canceled your zip line too. I'm sorry."

"What?" Z hollered. "We were *melting* out there!"

"How?" Dad looked at Jenn and Z, as if they could explain it. "Why?"

Ava faced Jenn. "I put dirt and rocks in your shoes." She turned to Dad. "The glitter…"

"I knew it," Z said with a hop.

"Ava. What…what…" Dad shook his head, as if he couldn't find the words to continue.

"I broke your glasses too. Not on purpose, though."

She couldn't say the next part.

It was too awful.

Pretend Mouse nudged her leg.

José whispered in her ear: *Everything is connected.*

Remember your good heart, Kylie said.

Dad crossed his arms. "Are you done?"

Ava shook her head. "I tried…" She couldn't…

"What?" Dad's voice was loud. "You tried what, Ava?"

"To get Rodrigo and Jenn back together."

Z made a choked sound. Jenn shut her eyes. Dad paced toward the door.

"I'm sorry." Ava covered her face with her hands.

"What in the name of Sam Hill has gotten into you?" Dad marched back to the desk. "Look at me, Ava. When did you get so selfish? So deceitful?"

"I—I don't know." It felt as if a fist were punching her heart, and she deserved it.

"You lied to me," Dad said. "You lied to all of us, again and again."

Ava nodded, which sent fat tears dripping onto her T-shirt.

Dad thudded across the wooden floor, back and forth. "It's like I don't even know you!"

It sounded like he didn't want to, either.

"Eric," Jenn said softly.

"You know what, Jenn?" Dad stopped mid-stride. "It seems I don't know you, either."

Jenn's mouth formed a tiny *o*.

"This is her fault!" Z pointed at Ava. "She wanted to ruin our vacation, and she did!"

"Mackenzie," Jenn gasped.

Z whirled around. "I bet you loved being partners with her, didn't you?"

"You didn't want to be with me," Jenn said.

Z waved her arms. "The two of you with your special costumes and your stupid friendship bracelets."

Now someone was kicking Ava's stomach.

"I bet you were so happy when Eric wanted to be my partner," Z continued. "So you didn't have to."

"Honey," Jenn said gently, "I thought it would be nice for

you and Eric to spend time together. But you wanted to be with Rodrigo from the beginning. It's not that I—"

"I want to *live* with him too. I'm older now," Z continued, as if challenging Jenn to disagree. "It's my choice. You'll be busy with the new baby anyway."

"Z," Dad said, "that's not fair."

Jenn turned to Dad. "Please don't correct my daughter."

"Got it." Dad raised his hands and dropped them. "You don't need me for much of anything, do you, Jenn?"

The color drained from Jenn's cheeks. "We need to talk." Her voice was hard as granite. She strode to the door.

"Seems like we should have done that sooner," Dad said.

"Well, gee, Eric," Jenn said, her hand on the doorknob, "since I didn't pack my magical time machine that's not an option."

Standing at the open hermitage door, Dad pointed at Ava. "You," he said, "are grounded." Then he dashed into the rain after Jenn, slamming the door.

Chart of Anger

	Ava	Z	Dad	Jenn
Is Ava mad at...	YES, YES, YES	Yep	SUPER MAD	NO
Is Z mad at...	Yes	?	YES	YES YES YES
Is Dad mad at...	SUPER MAD	Yes	No, he thinks he's right about everything.	YES YES YES
Is Jenn mad at...	Yes	Possibly	YES	?

CHAPTER 28

Z stood at the window, watching their parents sprint to the tent through the gray rain. "You weren't sick on Monday," she said.

It wasn't a question.

"I'm really sorry." Ava joined Z at the window. Her throat ached. She longed to tell Z about her anxiety. It wouldn't excuse her behavior, but it might explain it, at least a little.

"You made me think..." Z bit her lip and looked away. "I thought they might get back together. That's the only thing I've wanted for-*ev*-er."

"I'm so sorry," Ava whispered.

It was a song she couldn't stop singing.

Z was already out the door, and Ava chased her.

The rain still fell, but fortunately there was no thunder or lightning.

With her long legs, Z quickly passed the tent and crossed the clearing.

Ava jogged after her, skidding on the slick, wet grass. "Z! Wait! Please!"

The trail was Mud Run 2.0, a mountainous, soupy Slip 'N Slide, with bonus sharp rocks and roots. The rain and heavy clouds made them difficult to see too. It was only afternoon, but Ava wished she'd worn her headlamp.

Z, an otherworldly forest sprite, glided down the mountain, disappearing along the goopy path. A flutter of panic rose in Ava's chest, and for a millisecond, she considered turning back. She didn't want to be on the trail alone. Plus: She was grounded.

But she had to make things right with Z.

Keep going, Ava told herself. You're okay. Don't leave the trail. Don't think about wild animals. Don't get monkey brain. She plowed on, listening for danger—a snake's warning rattle or a seven-hundred-pound elk crashing through the brush. She heard only creaking trees in the wind, the patter of rain, and the usual hum-buzz-chirp-rustle-squeak of the forest.

And then: "Stop following me, Ava Headly!"

It was a relief to know she was on the right path, a little behind Z.

"I'm really, *really* sorry," Ava shouted. "Can we please talk?"

The wind and rain were the only reply.

Ava emerged from the trail, wet and muddy. She jogged around the lodge to the front. Down the road, a girl walked in the rain, her long, dark-purple hair plastered to her back.

Ava caught up with Z outside the art building. "Tell me how..." She pressed a hand to her chest and tried to catch her breath. "I can make it...up...to you."

Z looked at her coldly. "The damage is done." She marched down the road, yelling over her shoulder. "Stop following me, I said!"

"It's a free country," Ava yelled, trailing Z like a puppy. She had to prove how sorry she was, and that meant not giving up on trying to make it right. At least the rain had finally stopped.

Z entered the pool gate. A lifeguard whistled, signaling the few swimmers that they could return to the water. Z strutted toward the diving board as if saying: Bet you won't follow me now.

But Ava wove around kids and teenagers, making her way toward the deep end.

Z sauntered right past the diving board, though. Maybe she was circling the pool? After all, she was in street clothes.

Except...

Ava's breath caught.

No.

Noooooooo.

With a triumphant sneer, Z took her place in line for the high dive. She crossed her arms and popped a hip as if to say: It's official. You're a scaredy-cat baby. Not to mention a mean, scheming, lying Iowan.

Ava's mouth went dry. The high dive was unthinkably, unbearably high. Higher even than the Tower of Doom. Although, it hadn't been that bad.

But the high dive? She couldn't do it. She knew it. Z knew it. Everyone who had been at the pool yesterday knew it too.

So why was Ava still walking toward the deep end, past the

scary regular diving board, the site of her shame, to the even-more-treacherous high dive? Why was Ava acting like a person who was going to climb that tall, tall ladder, walk that narrow, springy plank, and jump—in her muddy clothes, which was totally against pool rules. Plus: Kids under thirteen weren't allowed to swim without an adult.

Surely a lifeguard would stop them.

One blew a whistle at some kids dunking each other, and the other deep-end lifeguard seemed to be flirting with another lifeguard.

Ava stepped into line behind Z. "I really am sorry," she whispered. "I know it was awful." No, that wasn't right, wasn't enough.

"*I* was awful," Ava corrected.

Only two people, a teenage boy and a little girl, stood between them and the board. The teenager scrambled up.

Ava wanted so badly to find the right words to make Z understand how truly sorry she was. "I thought if everyone had a bad time…if our parents broke up…. I was feeling awful too. I didn't think about how you'd feel. I was so selfish…"

Z didn't turn around, but she seemed to be listening. The teenager entered the water with a shout and splash, and the young girl scrambled up the ladder.

"I'd never want to hurt you, Z. I know I did, and I'm so sorry. I was so scared, but I'm going to do better. Be braver."

Z turned and met Ava's eyes.

"If you really want to change," she said, raising her chin toward the high dive, "prove it."

Ava didn't think jumping off the high dive would prove any-thing to Z. But in a weird way, it felt like—maybe—Ava could prove something to herself.

Here's what she knew: She didn't have to do it, even though Z was. Or even though Z had dared her, basically. In fact, if Z did something dangerous, Ava definitely shouldn't copy her.

The real question: Was the high dive dangerous?

What if it were merely scary? Could Ava do it? Did she want to? And if she didn't, was that only because she was scared? And was that a good reason?

Because: Ava was so tired of feeling afraid, tired of the head monkeys bossing her around.

Getting hurt on the high dive was possible, but it wasn't prob-able, was it? José had said the Tower of Doom would be bad for business if people were getting hurt every five minutes. Ava hadn't seen one person injured on the high dive.

The little girl stepped onto the board and, like an Olympian, executed a beautiful dive.

Why weren't the lifeguards blasting their whistles at Ava and Z? Why wasn't some nosy grownup freaking out and saying, "You kids can't be here in muddy street clothes! You don't look thirteen! Where are your irresponsible parents?"

Z was halfway up the ladder.

"Hey!" A lifeguard whistled at her. "Get down!"

Z shot along the board and jumped with a hair-raising whoop.

Ava raced up the ladder as Z passed her on the way down. The lifeguard blew his whistle.

At the top, Ava gripped the smooth rails and hoisted herself onto the board. She remembered what José had said about the Tower of Doom—it was like climbing a ladder. Wasn't the diving board like…walking? How many times had Ava fallen over while walking?

Zero.

She wasn't going to think about what had happened on the low dive.

Because: This was a new day.

She had defeated the Tower of Doom. After going back to help Z.

She had spoken up to help Jenn and her baby. Her and Dad's baby.

She had told the truth—about all the horrible things she'd done—even though she'd been so scared.

She wasn't perfect, she'd never be, but Ava was changing—like the mountains and everything else.

"Get down!" The lifeguard's voice came from far, *far* below. Ava didn't look.

She skit-skittered along the board—eyes straight ahead on the mountains—and, without stopping, plugged her nose and flung herself into the thin Colorado air.

The lifeguard's whistle shrieked as she fell. In an instant, her tennis shoes burst through the water, along with the rest of her. Ava paddled and kicked to the surface—and laughed.

"Yay, Ava," Z shouted, bobbing in the water near the side.

"Out of the pool, girls," the lifeguard said.

Ava's stomach rolled. Other than her recent grounding, she'd never really been in trouble. Could the lifeguard arrest them? What if he called the police?

Fortunately, a stern lecture was their only punishment, and after promising to never swim in street clothes, especially muddy ones, again—and to always swim with an adult until they turned thirteen—the girls were allowed to leave. Muddy water ran from their clothes and squished in their shoes. How much of this day had Ava spent wet and muddy?

"If someone bet me a million bucks that you'd jump," Z said, "I would have lost a million bucks."

"Me too," Ava said, and they laughed.

They walked toward the main lodge, silent except for the squelch of their shoes.

"Uh-oh," Z said.

Dad walked toward them. To say he looked unhappy would be like describing the mountains as a pile of pebbles.

"I know I'm probably double-grounded," Ava said. "But I can explain."

"We're leaving," Dad said. "You need to pack."

CHAPTER 29

They caught up with Dad behind the lodge.

"What happened?" Ava asked.

Dad shook his head. "Jenn wants to leave." He didn't even ask why they were soaking wet.

"Leave the resort?" Ava said. "Now?"

"As soon as possible."

"We have four more days," Z said as they started up the trail. "Are we going home?"

"You are." Dad sounded tired. "I'm going to try to change our flight so we can too."

Ava and Z exchanged a look. She'd be leaving Colorado almost a week early.

"What happened," Ava asked.

Dad sighed. "That's all I'm going to say right now."

"But, Dad, is Jenn—"

"Ava, I need you to not talk for a minute. Okay?"

But Ava, who so often had to force herself to speak, apparently couldn't be quiet now that that was the only thing Dad wanted from her. "Did you guys break up?"

When he didn't answer, Ava reached for his hand and was grateful, so grateful, he accepted it.

Ava had wanted them to break up. She had tried to break them up. But now that it might have happened, she felt worse than awful.

Was there a name for *that* feeling?

———————————————

They found Jenn at the hermitage, packed and ready to go. Plus: snoring.

She sprawled in the rocker, head back, legs akimbo, arms curled around her middle.

Dad raised an index finger in the "shhhh" sign. He pointed to their wet clothes and pantomimed that they should—quietly—go to the tent and change.

Ava could barely hold her tongue until she and Z were alone. "Did they break up?"

"I can't believe Mom wants to leave early," Z said.

Z had grabbed dry clothes in the hermitage, but not a towel. Ava handed her one.

With her own towel, she wiped her watch. She hoped the pool water hadn't hurt it. "What about the baby?" Ava said. "We've got to help them."

"We don't even know what's wrong."

Ava pressed her hands into her hair. It smelled like chlorine, and she wished she'd been able to shower. "They need to talk," she said, tugging off her wet shirt.

"Isn't that what they were doing in here?" Z said, but not unkindly. "What are we supposed to do—kidnap them, tie them up, and make them talk more?"

Ava pulled on a shirt. She waited until she popped out of the head hole to say, "Be serious."

"Do you think they'll get married?" Z asked.

"They don't even want to spend the rest of the week together."

"My mom and I don't get along *now*." Z stood at the tent entrance, her clothes dripping. "What's going to happen when she has a baby?"

"Did you mean what you said before? About living with Rodrigo?"

"'Tcha," Z made a disgusted sound. "Truth?"

Ava raised her towel from her face and nodded.

"I only see him a few times a year. Besides, you know, on TV."

"He lives in Colorado!" Hanging with Rodrigo here was all Z had talked about.

"He's busy."

Ava didn't know what to say. She visited Dad's parents twice a year, but they lived in Florida. She'd grown up without a mom, but it wasn't like her mother was too busy to see her.

"When did they get divorced?"

"You know what my first memory is?" Z said. "Playing rocket with Rodrigo. It was just a big cardboard box. We'd get in—he barely fit. We'd act like we were seeing all these cool space things. Like, my mom was an alien." Z smiled a sad, small smile. "I was four when he left."

Ava straightened. Rodrigo wasn't all bad, just like she wasn't. "You know what, Z? He looked really sad today when he said he had to leave early."

Z shook her head.

"You couldn't see him like I could," Ava insisted. "He looked like he was going to cry."

"He was making jokes."

"I think he wanted to hide his feelings, maybe."

Z crossed her arms.

"Seriously," Ava said.

"Why would he do that?"

"Maybe he didn't want you to feel worse? Or maybe he thinks he has to act cool because he's famous?" Maybe, like Ava, he wasn't even sure what he was feeling most of the time? "I bet he was really looking forward to seeing you too."

They were quiet for a moment.

"I always hoped they'd get back together." Z bent over and wrapped her hair in the towel.

"I made you think they were." Ava hadn't thought it was possible to feel worse.

"Not really."

"But you said—"

"I was mad." Z waved a hand. "I wanted to believe it."

It was the same, Ava realized, for her and the pregnancy test sticks. She'd done everything she could to convince herself that Dad had had nothing to do with it.

"You tried," Z said with her uneven shrug. "They hate each other."

"They love you."

Just like Dad loved Ava. But he also loved Jenn, and Ava had tried to destroy that. What kind of monster tried to kill love? What if Dad had tried to break up Ava, Kylie, and Emma's friendship? It wasn't the same, but it would have been unbelievably cruel.

"I didn't think about how I was messing with them—our parents—and with Rodrigo and you, with everybody's happiness." Ava dried her feet. "I did so many bad things—"

"A lot a lot," Z agreed, finally removing her wet clothes. "Why did you tell us, though?"

"I don't know." Ava swallowed. "It felt like I'd hurt you—all of you—even if you never found out." She looked up at Z. "But I was so afraid you'd hate me."

Z's expression softened. "Being mad and hating aren't the same."

Ava had never thought about that. "Thanks for not hating me."

"I'm still mad, though."

Ava nodded. She would've felt the same. "I'm not usually like that in real life—"

"Real life." Z snorted.

"When I got here, I think I sort of forgot who I was."

"You helped me at the Mud Run. That's a big deal. Most people wouldn't have, Ava. Lots of people passed me before you got there."

"I wanted to beat you so bad too." Had Z seen Rodrigo taking selfies with fans? "Did you know Rodrigo was coming?"

"To the Mud Run? No. He said he had some free time and wanted to see me. He was probably feeling guilty about the other night. He said he forgot about the Mud Run."

"It was cool he did it with you anyway," Ava said. "Should I tell him it was my fault you weren't here on Monday?"

"That's okay."

"Your mom loves you," Ava said. "You should talk to her."

"Man, you're all about talking lately." Z suddenly grinned. "Did you really put dirt and rocks in her shoes? That's so random."

"And immature." Ava's cheeks warmed as she remembered Z's words at the campfire.

"You don't really act like you're thirty," Z said. "I wish you'd told me about the glitter, though. We could have gotten my mom too. And I really am sorry for saying you're no fun. I shouldn't have said that. It's not true, either."

"Thanks." Ava wasn't going to apologize for promoting fire safety, but she still had more apologizing to do. "Remember that first day at lunch? I said you were stupid if you didn't know how dangerous Colorado was?"

"You got a time-out." Z snickered.

"Like a three-year-old." Ava hid her face. "I was so mad at him." She dropped her hands so she could look Z in the eye. "I took it out on you, which is terrible. I really did want to apologize to you then—a real one, not just say 'sorry,' in a snotty way?"

Z nodded.

"But when my dad told me to…"

"Yeah. It's okay. By the way, I'd say you act more like twenty-seven or, maybe even twenty-six"—she arched an eyebrow—"and a half."

Ava smiled. It wasn't the first time someone had pointed out that, perhaps, she worried about things beyond her years. Z had said it in her funny Z way.

"I don't think you're stupid," Ava said. "Not at all."

Unable to keep herself in Iowa or even Denver, Ava had felt powerless. But she'd ruined everyone's vacation and maybe even helped break up Dad and Jenn. Maybe she was more powerful than she'd realized? If that were true, maybe she could do some good.

"We need to help them." Ava whispered in case a Dad-shaped shadow appeared outside the tent. "Maybe we could force them to talk more."

"We're back to kidnapping?" Z said.

But Ava was already forming a plan. Could she do it? For real? She turned to Z. "We have to convince them that we need to eat supper before we leave. Say you're starving or—"

"I am."

"Good. We also need to get your mom's car keys."

"Ava! You can't even see over the steering wheel!"

"I don't have a license! How unsafe is that?" Ava shook her head with frustration.

Z stared at her with that lopsided grin.

"What?" Ava said.

"You're trying to stay in the mountains."

"What?" Ava repeated because, apparently, it had become her favorite word. "No, I'm…"

"You are!" Z jumped up, laughing, and dancing around. "You, Ava Louise Headly," she said, pointing, "are plotting to stay in the mountains!"

CHAPTER 30

Jenn's eyes were red when the girls entered the cabin. Ava hoped it was from allergies but suspected crying.

Z hugged her mom. "Can we eat dinner before we leave? Please? I'm so hungry."

"Me too," Ava said.

"Hmm." Jenn shut her eyes, and her head bobbled against the rocker.

"It's been a long, tough day," Dad said. "Why don't you rest a bit more? I'll get the girls supper, and then we can go. I'll get something for you to eat in the car."

Dad guided Jenn to the bed, and she crawled under the covers fully dressed. Meanwhile, Z lifted Jenn's keys from her purse and smiled at Ava. Dad didn't realize he'd helped their plan.

"Why does Jenn want to leave?" Ava asked as they started down the muddy trail for the gizillionth time that day.

"She's over it," Dad said.

"Over what?" Ava hoped it wasn't them.

Dad sighed. "The Mud Run, Rodrigo, sleeping in a twin bed with Z in that tiny cabin without electricity or running water, rocks and dirt in her shoes…" He looked pointedly at Ava. "It would be a lot even if you weren't hormonal."

"What's hormonal?"

Dad shifted his backpack. "Chemicals that control body functions. If they get out of whack—like when a woman is pregnant—that affects someone's mood."

"Jenn's in a bad mood because she's going to have a baby?" Ava asked.

"I didn't say—"

"She's been in a bad mood a lot," Z said. "A lot a lot."

"Her body is working hard," Dad said. "She's making a whole human."

"Did you break up?" Z asked.

"No." Dad stopped abruptly, removed his broken glasses, and rubbed his eyes. "But we're working through some things."

"What things?" Z pressed.

"That's between us." He smiled at them. "The important thing is that you two are going to be awesome big sisters."

"I'll be the biggest sister, though," Z said, giving Ava a mischievous grin.

Ava smiled. It was true. Z was older and taller.

"Are you getting married?" Z asked as they resumed walking.

"I'd like to," Dad said. "But I don't know."

"Would you live together?" Z continued.

"Well, yeah."

"But where?"

"Oh." Dad stopped again. Even though Z had asked, his eyes met Ava's. "You and I would move to Colorado, Baby Ava Girl."

Chills squigged up Ava's back, to her neck and into her ears. Her stupid, stupid ears that had betrayed her by hearing those words:

Move. To. Colorado.

This was the cold fear that had wafted like a ghost in the back of her mind since she'd discovered the pregnancy-test sticks, way too scary to consider or even name. Even when she'd wondered if Jenn was pregnant and if she and Dad would get married, even when Kylie brought up moving, it hadn't felt truly possible.

Now, Dad basically was saying (without saying): It was probable.

"Why can't they move to Iowa?"

"Jenn and Rodrigo have a legal agreement that they'll both stay in Colorado."

"But he never sees her." Ava gripped her watch.

"Jenn also has a good job here that she loves," Dad said. "I'm portable."

"But Mouse—"

"He'd come with us."

"But not...." Not Grandmom. Not Granddad. Not Uncle Steve. Not Mrs. Mendez. Not Kylie. Not Emma. Not Kylie's mom. Not everyone she'd known her whole life.

"They'd visit," Dad said, "and we'd visit them."

Ava sniffed. She wanted to rush back, rouse Jenn, leave Colorado, and never, ever return.

Dad squeezed her shoulder. "You have to remember, no one's getting married right now. We have some issues to work through."

––––––––––––

"I've got to pee," Z announced, midway through supper.

Those were the code words to launch their secret Stay-in-the-Rockies-So-Our-Parents-Can-Talk-More plan. But they'd made that plan before Ava knew—really, for-sure knew—Dad's ultimate plan: to move them to Colorado.

Ava looked away.

"Ava?" Z kicked her under the table. "Don't you need to go to the bathroom?"

When Ava didn't answer, Z jostled her shoulder.

Ava turned. "I'm okay."

Z quirked an eyebrow and stood. "Come with, anyway," she ordered, grabbing Ava's arm.

Ava finally stood. Just because she left with Z didn't mean she had to carry out the plan. "We'll be right back," she told Dad.

Ava allowed Z to hustle her through the lodge and out to the parking lot.

"We need to be quick," Z said, glancing around, as if they were about to steal the car.

Ava looked at her sandals. "I kind of don't want to."

"You said it wouldn't hurt the car!"

"It won't." Ava finally looked at Z.

"Are you worried about getting in trouble?" Z's eyes narrowed. "This was your idea."

Ava tried to sound casual. "I don't feel like it anymore."

"But why?"

Ava shrugged.

"Tell me what to do," Z said. "I'll do it."

"Why do you want to fix this so bad?" Ava said. "None of this is your fault. Do you even like your mom?"

Z jerked back. "I love my mom. What's going on with you?"

If Ava succeeded in helping Dad make up with his sweetheart, he'd force her to leave everyone and everything she loved. She sniffed again, fighting the tears threatening to come.

"What's wrong?" Z asked, kinder.

Ava shook her head and turned. Stupid, stupid tears. Stupid Colorado.

"Ohhh," Z said. "You don't want them to get married."

Ava turned back. "I do," she said, wiping her eyes. "Sort of."

If Dad and Jenn got married, Ava would have a mom. Not a regular one, either—a great one. She and Z would be sisters. And then, the baby would be born...in Colorado.

"How can you want two things at the same time?" Ava asked. "Opposite things?"

"You just do." Z shrugged her lopsided shrug. "You know Eric's probably called the police to report us missing, right?"

In her mind, Ava saw Dad's quick smile when Jenn entered the room, how he took her hand for no reason, their hushed conversations punctuated with loud laughter. He loved her. And Ava loved Dad.

Ava held out her hand like a surgeon asking for a scalpel. "Keys."

Once Ava pulled the hood release inside the Jeep, she pressed and pushed everything she could reach under the Jeep's narrowly raised hood. "There's a latch that opens it," she explained, peering into the dark space. "Somewhere."

"Ow," Z said, cramming both hands into the space. "This is so awkward!"

"I know."

"I'm trying to move anything that could maybe be a latch but—"

"I know."

"Nothing's happening." Z slapped the Jeep's hood. "Ow."

"Don't kick the tires," Ava warned.

Z shook out her hands. "What about Eric? Maybe he—"

"Are you joking? I'm already in so much trouble."

"He doesn't want to leave either."

Z was right. If they couldn't open the hood, the four of them would leave tonight. Dad would be crushed.

"Come on," Ava said, already jogging to the lodge.

As they entered the cafeteria, Dad rose to meet them. "What are you trying to do to me?"

"We need your help," Z said.

"You need my help going to the ladies' room?"

Ava looked at her feet.

"Did you lie again?" He paused. "Ava?"

"It's a secret plan," Z explained, "but we need help."

"You lied to me so you could do a secret plan?" He bent over. "Look at my hair!"

Z stood on tiptoe. "What am I looking for? Dandruff?"

"Am I going gray?" Dad straightened. "I must be, trying to keep up with you two."

Dad had made a joke! That was a good sign.

"Come on," Z said, pulling him out of the cafeteria and to the Jeep, as she'd done with Ava. "Can you open the hood?"

Dad frowned. "Why do you need to do that?"

"There's a thing I need to do," Ava said.

"Oh, then, sure. Let me help you out." Dad, hands on his hips, didn't move.

Ava looked at Z.

"I'm not going to do anything unless—look at me, Ava—unless I know what it is."

"She's going to make the Jeep not start," Z blabbed.

"Ava! You can't hurt Jenn's car."

"I'm going to take out the fuel pump fuse."

"But—"

"So you guys can talk. So Jenn won't make us leave."

Even though leaving would be best for Ava. Even though she'd wanted to leave since before she'd arrived.

Dad stared as if she were green and had floated off a spaceship. "Let me understand." He removed his glasses and pinched his nose between his eyes. "If you take that thing out, the Jeep won't start?" He returned his glasses to his face. He really needed new ones.

"Right."

"And you can put it back in, and it'll start?"

"Yes."

"You're absolutely sure?"

"Yes."

Pretty sure.

"It's not dangerous? You're not touching any wires?"

"No. It's a fuse."

Dad nodded once, turned, and opened the hood.

It took only a moment for Ava to study the diagram inside, like she'd seen online. A second later, she plucked out the Jeep's fuel pump fuse.

Dad slammed the hood. "Where on Earth did you learn that, Baby Ava Girl?"

Ava smiled. "The internet."

Dad wrapped his arm around Ava and gave her a sideways hug. Then the three of them walked back to the lodge, where Dad bought Jenn a sandwich and had the girls store it in their bathhouse locker until they were ready to leave. When they finally returned to the cabin, though, Jenn was conked out.

"Maybe she won't want to leave tomorrow?" Ava whispered on the porch.

Z held up crossed fingers.

Even though it wasn't close to his usual bedtime, Dad yawned. "I've got to get some shut-eye too," he said.

It had been the world's longest day, and Ava was tired. But what if she and Dad went home tomorrow? When would she see Z again? "Can I sit out here with Z for a while?"

Dad looked surprised but nodded. "Not too late, though." He started toward the tent but pivoted back. "Ava? Do not leave camp and don't wake up Jenn."

"I won't."

"No more secret plots, either."

"I know."

"I'll keep an eye on her," Z said, slinging an arm around Ava's shoulders.

"Oh, that makes me feel much better," Dad said, but he smiled.

"And I'll keep an eye on her." Ava had to stretch on tiptoe to wrap an arm around Z's shoulders, which cracked them up. But they quickly hushed. Because: Jenn.

"You two are quite the team," Dad said.

"We've got it covered," Ava agreed. "A to Z."

CHAPTER 31

When Dad finally retreated to the tent, Ava and Z settled onto the hermitage's uneven steps. The surrounding peaks glowed violet in the sun's dying light. "Purple mountain majesties," Ava said, pointing. "Like that song."

"The woman who wrote 'America the Beautiful' was inspired by Pike's Peak." Z quirked an eyebrow. Maybe she could teach Ava to do that someday? "That's in Colorado, Ava."

"We sing that in school," Ava said. "The beginning always makes me think of Iowa—spacious skies and amber waves of grain."

"You really love Iowa."

"Yep." Who wouldn't?

"Why do you hate Colorado, though?" Z's jiggling foot rocked the porch slightly.

"I don't."

"Colorado is one of the most popular states."

"Z, I don't hate it." It went beyond simply not hating, though. "I like Colorado. But it has a lot *a lot* of dangers." Since meeting Z, she thought one "a lot" seemed inadequate. "And I..."

Could she finally tell? For some reason Ava didn't understand, it seemed important for Z to know, even if she laughed or thought Ava was weird.

"I have anxiety."

Z's foot stilled. "What do you mean?"

"My doctor says it's like having a broken smoke detector."

"Huh?"

"She says everyone has a smoke detector inside them—not a real one, obviously." Ava laughed a strange non-laugh. "It tells you when there's danger. It keeps you safe." She glanced at Z, who nodded. "But some people have extra-sensitive alarms, I guess." Ava squeezed her palms between her knees. "Their alarms go off even when there's no fire."

"So," Z said, "you always feel like you're in danger?"

"Not always. But yeah."

"That would suck. Big time."

"Yeah." Z understood—and she didn't seem to be judging.

"I have ADHD," Z said.

"Really?" Ava hadn't imagined that Z might have something challenging to deal with too. But now that she thought about it—Z's constant motion, the interesting way her mind worked—ADHD made sense. Ava thought of Emma back home.

"One of my best friends has that," Ava said. "Do you have a hard time in school? Because of the sitting?"

"So much sitting," Z groaned. On cue, she rose and bounced on her toes. "But my teachers have been pretty cool about letting me move around." She swung her arms.

"That's good." Ava cleared her throat. "My anxiety is probably why I don't do things…why I'm a…you know…a scaredy-cat. Like you said."

Z jumped over the stairs to the ground and faced Ava. "I never said that."

"Are you kidding?"

"When?"

"Yesterday! To those girls at the pool."

"I didn't mean—"

"When we first saw the hermitage and when I wouldn't dye my hair."

"Oh." Z's arms stilled. "Sorry."

"It's true, though. I hate it." Ava met Z's eyes. "I sort of wanted to dye my hair, though."

That got a small smile. "You're not a scaredy-cat, Ava. Not a hundred percent."

Ava shook her head. Z was trying to be nice.

"You did the Mud Run, right? You saved me from the Tower of Doom!" Z reached behind herself and grabbed one of her ankles, which she pulled high above her head. She had excellent balance. "I still can't believe you went off the high dive!"

"Me, either!" Ava giggled. "It was…it was fun." The word didn't feel so painful between them anymore. "But, Z, I was terrified."

Z lowered her leg and scowled. "Have you learned nothing from the Zorn Chronicles?"

"I haven't gotten that far," Ava admitted.

"You know how it ends." Z's expression left no doubt about her feelings on that. "Being brave doesn't mean you're not scared, Ava. Brave people are scared all the time, but they do the right thing anyway, like risking their lives to rescue the Book of Ga'an."

Was Z right? Could someone be scared and brave at the same time?

"You know what?" Z frowned and stared toward the jagged horizon, dark against the dying light. Usually, her words were like a stream in springtime, full to the banks and rushing with melted snow. But she seemed to be working something out, like in a mystery novel just before the amateur detective finally says, "Aha! The killer's identity is obvious."

Z slowly walked up the steps and sat beside Ava. "I just thought of this. I don't think it's possible to be brave without being scared."

"What do you mean?" The temperature had dropped with the sun, and Ava tucked her arms inside her T-shirt and wrapped them around her middle.

"It's almost like being scared is a requirement. Because if you're not, it's no biggie, right?" Z said. "You only have to be brave when you're scared."

Ava nodded slowly. This made sense. The Tower of Doom and the high dive had been one kind of scary. But admitting the horrible things she'd done had been so much worse.

"I was scared to tell you the truth," Ava said, "but I did!"

"No scaredy-cat would have done that," Z said.

"Oh, no." Ava groaned and lowered her head to her knees. Her arms were still trapped inside her T-shirt. "I remembered something else I need to tell you."

"What?" Z sounded wary, and Ava didn't blame her.

"This is so stupid." Ava sat up. "I—I haven't gotten my period yet."

"Huh?"

"You asked, remember? You said you hadn't gotten yours yet, and that made me feel good, in a way, like I wasn't alone, because my two best friends got theirs this year." Ava looked at Z. "But then… I lied. I guess I thought you'd think I was more mature. Not a baby."

"That's messed up," Z said.

"Yeah." Ava smiled. That's what Emma would have said.

"What does Eric call you? Ava girl baby?"

"Girl baby? No!"

Z joined in Ava's laughter. "Something-baby, though."

Giggling, Ava glanced at the hermitage door. She hoped Jenn was a sound sleeper. "*Baby Ava Girl*. It's completely different." Ava wiped her laugh-tears through her T-shirt.

"He won't let me get a phone," Ava said. "At least Rodrigo knows you're growing up and stuff."

"Did you see his fans today?" Z bounced in place. "It's insane how super-famous he is."

"Yeah."

"Does your dad have anxiety too?"

Ava faced Z. "Why would you say that?"

"I don't mean it in a bad way." Z shrugged. "He's obsessed with sunscreen."

"He's only scared of pickles and spiders. And you should wear sunscreen every day, Z. You don't want skin cancer."

"Your dad's afraid of pickles?"

"He's allergic."

The sun had sunk behind the mountains, and it was growing darker. The usual strange sounds echoed from the forest. Ava allowed herself only one scan for glittering wild-animal eyes. She didn't want to rile up her monkeys before bed.

Z looked at Ava. "I know your dad bugs you," she said, "and, yeah, he's nerdy—and not in the cool way, but in the dad way."

"For sure."

"And those glasses."

"Ugh." The tape was horrible. Ava couldn't help feeling guilty.

"Right?" Z said. "But he's a good dad."

"Yeah." Ava had always known this, and Rodrigo had only helped her appreciate Dad more. At the same time, something wasn't quite right between them. Ava had wanted to blame Colorado, but whatever it was, it had started a while ago. The trip had only made it more obvious. Ava glanced up. "Oh!"

It looked as if someone had tossed silver glitter onto the vast, black-velvet sky, a nighttime God wink.

Z followed her gaze. "Yowza."

"You might drive a rocket up there some day," Ava said.

"That will be epic." Z smiled.

"Do you think that rocket game with Rodrigo is why?"

"Oh. Huh. Maybe?" She looked at Ava. "What do you really want to do when you grow up? It's not—what did you say before?—a lion tamer?"

"Ha! No. I want to be a librarian or a teacher." Ava touched her watch. "Or an actor."

"It would be cool to be around books all day. I still think you'd be an excellent spy."

Spying didn't interest Ava, but with Z, she'd learned not to rule out anything.

"Ava?" Dad's voice carried from the darkness.

Both girls shrieked. Z clutched Ava, whose arms still were pinned inside her T-shirt, and they tumbled onto the porch, dissolving into relieved laughter. Ava wiggled her arms free.

"I thought you were Bigfoot," Z said.

"Sorry! I didn't mean to startle you." Dad rubbed the back of his neck. "Are you ready to turn in, Baby Ava Girl? I can't seem to fall asleep with you out here."

Ava and Z shared a look. Maybe Dad had more worries than Ava realized?

They stood as Dad walked back to the tent.

"Ava?"

"Yeah?"

"If I was going to have a sister, I'd want her to be like you."

Ava smiled at Z. "Same."

CHAPTER 32

"Dad?" Ava's heart banged as she changed into her nightgown inside the tent. Kylie had encouraged her to talk to him, and Ava knew now she needed to. It felt scary, though, to tell him she was mad. What if he got mad back? But being mad wasn't the same as hating someone. Dad might get mad, like Ava sometimes felt mad at him (a lot a lot lately).

But Dad would never, could never, do anything but love her. And now Ava knew feeling scared was the first step toward acting brave. "Can we talk?"

"I'm exhausted," he said, "and I'm sure you are too. Let's talk in the morning, okay?"

Ava crossed her arms. "You lied to me."

"Me?" Dad shook his head and looked up, as if asking God—or Ava's mom or the tent ceiling—can you believe this? "You're the one who's been lying, Ava Louise, which we definitely will discuss. Later."

"Why?"

"So we're thinking more clearly."

"No, I mean, why did I lie?"

He shook his head again, as if trying to get rid of a bad dream. "You're the only one who can answer that. You need to go to bed, Ava." He stretched out on his sleeping bag and pulled up his blanket. He hadn't slept inside it since the glitter incident.

"Because I..." She had to say it, even though it was embarrassing. "I was scared." She forced herself to look at him. "You knew I was scared, so you didn't tell me things. Maybe you thought you were protecting me." She shut her eyes for a second. She didn't want to hurt his feelings. "But you kind of made it worse." When he didn't respond, she continued, "You never told me things were so serious with Jenn."

"You didn't seem interested."

That was true. Ava hadn't paid much attention. "She lived so far away. Why didn't you make me listen? Like you make me tell you stuff sometimes even when I don't want to."

He smiled slightly.

"At Red Rocks you said babies were a long way off."

Dad sat up. "I thought that was the truth."

"You didn't even tell me you loved her. Dad, that's a big deal! You told me you"—Ava did air quotes—"*really liked* and *cared for* her. It's almost like you tell me some things only when you can't *not* tell me, Dad. Like, I only found out we might—"

She couldn't say "move."

"You're right. I'm sorry."

Ava appreciated the apology, but he needed to understand. "It's mean in a way," she continued, "and disrespectful, and please stop calling me Baby Ava Girl."

"What?" His voice squeaked. "Ava, I—"

"I'm growing up, but you won't…you don't—"

"I'm trying to protect you, Ava. Sometimes I think you're too smart for your own good. You don't realize you're still a child."

"I'm not a baby, though. Z has a cell phone."

Darn. How had that slipped out?

Dad crossed his arms. "Go to bed."

"No! I mean, yes, I want a cell phone. But it's bigger than that. You're not listening."

"I hear more than you probably realize. I hear how worried you are, Ava."

Ava sighed. "I don't know why I'm so…this way."

"Come here."

Even though she was a teenager, practically, Ava crawled onto his lap and leaned back against his chest. His strong arms felt good, circling her. "I wish so badly I could make it better for you," he whispered, lightly kissing the back of her head. "I know Field Day was horrible. I can't imagine how scary it was. But, in the end, I think it probably was good."

"Why?"

"Because now we know more about what's happening—and you're getting help."

"But if we move, I can't see Dr. C."

"Denver has many wonderful doctors."

They were quiet for a moment. The insects and night creatures serenaded them.

"Dad? Do you have anxiety?"

"I don't know." His arms tightened around her. "Maybe I'm a little overprotective. What happened to your mom—it was awful." His voice sounded thick. He exhaled slowly. "She was something else. Smart, funny, pretty. Strong and brave—and you're so much like her."

Dad thought she was brave? And strong, for real? Ava's arms and legs weren't muscle-y like Jenn's and Z's. But maybe there were different ways to be strong.

"She was so healthy…all through her pregnancy. The delivery went fine."

Ava held her breath. She'd never heard these details.

"She couldn't stop smelling your head."

Ava turned to look at him. "My head?"

Dad nodded, his smile sad. "You were two days old when we lost her." He blinked rapidly. "She had a bad headache, but we didn't think…Then she felt a little dizzy, and her legs started swelling." He coughed once. "We went to the ER…"

Ava hid her face in his neck.

"We were so young." Dad's voice was faint. He rubbed Ava's back. "And I knew nothing—less than zero—about babies." He took a big breath. "Your grandparents were heartbroken, of course. We all were. Grandmom, Granddad, and Uncle Steve love you so much—but they were grieving. They couldn't…You were only about a month old when we moved across the street from Mrs.

Mendez. She was there for us day and night, all those years. That woman is a living saint."

"Did you know her before we moved there?"

"No." Dad sniffed. "But your mom did."

That made sense. Dad hadn't grown up in the area like Ava's mom had.

"Mrs. Mendez and I talked about it once. She said there was some real ugliness in the community years ago."

"Really?" Ava couldn't imagine it. The only real division she'd seen was when her beloved Iowa State Cyclones played the University of Iowa Hawkeyes. "What happened?"

"There was a fight between a Latino kid and a white kid—I don't know what it was about, but, fortunately, neither was badly hurt. But, somehow, these hard feelings spread, and there were threats and lots of racism against the Latino community."

"That's terrible."

"Your mom was in high school. Did you know she graduated with Arturo, Mrs. Mendez's grandson?"

"No."

"They were part of this group…these teenagers who stood together against hate." Dad removed his glasses and wiped his eyes. "Mrs. Mendez said they showed the so-called grownups what was what. I think that's why…when we moved in and she found out your mom had passed, she did so much for us."

Ava began to cry. "How can you make us leave her?"

"It will be hard. But I love Jenn, Ava."

Dad pulled Ava from him and studied her face. "I already love our little baby, just like I loved you before you were born." He gently wiped Ava's tears. "Loving Jenn and the new baby, that doesn't mean I love you less. You know that, right?"

"Do you love Z?"

Dad smiled. "I do. But none of this means—I could never, ever love you less, Baby Ava Girl—oh, sorry. Ava." He cleared his throat. "I'll always love your mom too."

"But she's not here," Ava said. She wished she had known her mom. She turned and settled back against Dad's chest. It was getting hard to keep her eyes open.

"Dad?" Ava's voice was a small, soft squeak. "What if…" It was too terrible to say. But she had to know. She had to be brave. "What if Jenn dies too?"

"Oh, honey." He held her tighter.

"Did I…" Ava swallowed. Squeezed her eyes shut. "Did I kill Mom?"

"Oh, Ava, no! No!" Dad nudged her to turn around and he held her shoulders as his eyes searched hers. "Of course not! No." He sniffed and wiped his eyes. "It's no one's fault. Bad things happen sometimes. All we can do is love each other through it."

He hugged her, his shoulders shaking.

Ava woke to Dad's snores. She pulled on her tennis shoes and walked to the outhouse. The gauzy light was the same as the day before—had it only been yesterday that she and Jenn had crept away to prepare for the Mud Run?

Fluttery birds gossiped in the treetops and the cool air cut through

Ava's nightgown as she scurried to the "privy," as Grandmom called it. Grandmom had grown up with an outhouse before her own father, Ava's great-grandpa, installed indoor plumbing at the farm. The thought of leaving Grandmom—and everyone—was utterly unthinkable.

Ava's roots were there. They tied her to her mom and her mom's family.

But she also wanted Dad and Jenn to work out whatever was wrong. Maybe after a good sleep, Jenn would want to stay? If she didn't, the missing fuel pump fuse would make her.

The blast of freezing air on her privates remained an unwelcome surprise, no matter how many times Ava experienced it. But she hadn't seen any evidence of animals popping out of the toilet, so she'd mentally filed that worry under "not probable."

On her way back, she met Dad on the trail, heading toward the outhouse. "Good morning," he said, giving her a hug. "Did you sleep okay?"

"Yeah. Did you?"

"I did."

Ava glanced at the hermitage. "Do you want to do a short hike before they get up?"

A grin brightened his entire face. "I think this is the first time you've hiked voluntarily," he said. A few minutes later, they descended the narrow path toward the main trail. "You're so much more sure-footed," he said.

"Do you think Jenn will still want to leave?"

"I don't know."

"Aren't you worried?"

"There are things we've got to work out, but we will."

The trees rose high, on thin trunks. The lodgepole pines had brown bark with stiff, sharp emerald needles. The aspens' bark was greenish-white. Their fat teardrop leaves were bright green on top, light underneath. They fluttered in the breeze, catching the light like mini mirrors.

"I was trying to remember when you started going to the outhouse by yourself," Dad said. "Remember our first morning? Now, you run up there like it's nothing."

Why was he talking about outhouses? "What are the chances we'll move?" Ava tried to keep her voice steady. "Fifty-fifty?" She stepped over a large rock. "Ninety-nine to one?"

"Ava." Dad's eyes held hers. "I one hundred percent want to marry Jenn."

Ava swallowed. "And we'd one hundred percent move?"

"Yes."

"I don't want to."

"I know."

"It's not fair."

"I know." He gestured to a trail, shooting off the main one. "That goes to a waterfall. Should we check it out?"

"Is it taller than Minnehaha?" Ava liked visiting that waterfall when she and Dad vacationed in Minnesota's Twin Cities. She also loved saying its Dakota Sioux name.

"We'll have to see," Dad said.

The mountain air smelled clean and crisp, and faintly of pine.

The sky—Ava had never seen one so blue. She'd read about that, she suddenly remembered, on the Denver tourism website. The sky really was bluer, it said, because there was less water vapor in the air. Why hadn't she written that in her notebook? She liked the way the sunlight spilled onto the trail, interspersed with patchy shade. Of course, the sun's harmful UV rays were stronger here, but she was coated in sunscreen. She liked the tall trees, too, and the stillness.

She had a strange feeling in her chest, like fingers uncurling from a fist. Her shoulders—this was a nice surprise—felt loose and weren't reaching for her ears. And then, holy guacamole:

She felt good.

Here.

Now.

Even with everything messed up and the future unsure. The fresh air, rising sun, brilliant blue sky, and distant churn of tumbling water had buoyed Ava's mood like magic. She didn't have to do anything.

With the mountains I am one.

It was a line from the poet José was named after.

Everything is connected.

CHAPTER 33

"I've been thinking about what you said last night," Dad said as they began the new trail.

"What part?"

Dad gave her a small smile. "You said I only tell you things when I have to. That I've kept things from you, important things. I didn't realize I was doing that. No, that's not right. I waited to tell you a few things—"

"A lot a *lot* of things."

"What I didn't realize was why."

"Because I'll freak out."

"I don't like seeing you upset. But there's more to it." Dad stopped to tie his shoe. When he straightened, his eyes met Ava's. "I think it's because I'm scared too."

Ava sucked in her breath. If Dad was scared, Ava was scared. Maybe Z was right, and he had anxiety too? Where did that leave them?

"When you get upset, I want to make it better."

"But that's not your job," Ava said. They'd talked about this with Dr. C. at their last session. Everyone was responsible for their own feelings.

"I know. But I forget. I want to make you feel better, but I don't know how."

"Dr. C. said we can't control outside things," Ava said. "Only ourselves."

Dad smiled. "That's right. I guess I keep things from you so I don't have to deal with how you might feel about it." He took a long breath. "And that's not right. That's not fair."

"But, Dad—"

He raised a hand. "Let me finish, okay? Then I'll listen to whatever you need to say." He looked off into the distance for a moment before turning back. "I want to be a perfect dad, Ava, but I can't be. There's no such thing."

"We're all perfectly imperfect," Ava said. "That's what Jenn says."

"She does?" Dad took a breath. "You were so tiny. I thought I'd break you…"

"But you didn't."

"You're becoming a young woman." Dad's voice rose. "What do I know about that?"

"You're a great dad," Ava said. "I'm sorry I freak out."

"You haven't done anything wrong." Dad stopped. He searched her eyes. "It's okay to have your feelings, Baby Ava Girl. I should be encouraging you to feel them, not trying to control them. You were brave to tell me how you felt."

Of all the things Ava might have imagined she'd be good at, talking—especially about feelings—was last on the list. Just after being brave.

"I called you 'Baby Ava Girl.' I'm sorry."

"It's okay." It was like noticing her brain monkeys or thinking about probable versus possible or remembering to un-scrunch her shoulders. Habits were hard to change.

"I want to do better," Dad said as they resumed walking. "I'm going to find someone to help me with my worries too."

"You already know belly breathing."

"That's right." He laughed. "What if I called you sweet pickle? Would that be okay?"

Jenn said everything changes. Ava and Dad were changing too.

Ava didn't want to move. But if they did, it would bring good changes too. Just because she often felt anxious didn't mean she wasn't also brave and strong. She'd be okay, whatever happened, especially with support from Dad, Jenn, and Z.

The trail curved, revealing a veil of churning water, clear as tap water, rioting down a jumble of stair-step gray-black boulders. When Ava and Dad visited Minnehaha Falls, they'd stood with other photo-taking tourists. This felt as if they were the only two people on Earth.

"Look," she said. A rainbow shimmered in the spray. A God wink.

If their plan was successful, they wouldn't leave today. Still, that didn't mean Dad and Jenn would fix their problems.

Wanting something and not wanting it at the same time was awful.

When they returned from their hike, Z sailed off the porch and ran to them. "We're still going," she said. "Mom talked to the lodge people. They said to leave the tent."

"Thanks," Dad said. "We'll be ready in five minutes."

No one said what they all were thinking: Would the Jeep start? And: What then?

Jenn waited at the trailhead.

"Good morning," Dad said. When he leaned in for a kiss, she turned, and his lips brushed her cheek.

"Morning." Jenn's voice was as cool as the mountain air, and she set off down the trail.

Ava, wearing her novel-filled backpack, hurried after her. "Remember when I first hiked up this trail? It was so hard. I was really scared wild animals would eat us. Or I'd fall off the mountain. Or a boulder would fall on me."

"I remember."

"Or there'd be a storm," Ava continued, "with lightning."

"Careful." Jenn guided Ava around a pointy rock. "Your hiking has really improved in a short time, Ava."

"You helped me, Jenn." A lump grew in Ava's throat. Ava would miss Jenn if they left today. "A lot *a lot*."

Dad and Z were back a ways, sharing a laugh. Ava wasn't jealous. There was plenty of Dad goodness to go around, and Z deserved more than Rodrigo was able to give.

Ava turned back to Jenn. "I'm glad we were partners."

"Me too. You were right about my costume, though."

"I'm really sorry I blabbed, Jenn."

Jenn reached for Ava's hand. "Thank you for caring so much about me and the baby."

"I'm sorry I was so mean at the bracelet class. I don't know why I was. Because I—" She glanced at Jenn again. "I really like you. A lot a lot."

"I like you too, Ava," Jenn said. "A lot a lot *a lot*."

Ava smiled at the third "a lot," relieved Jenn didn't hate her. At least, not yet. "I shouldn't have put dirt and rocks in your shoes. I'm sorry."

"I forgive you. But please don't do it again."

"Why didn't you tell on me? About the glitter?"

Jenn smiled. "I just wish I could have gotten in on that action."

Ava laughed, then sobered. "Remember what I said about Dad's girlfriends?"

"Yes."

"That was a lie too. A huge one. I'm sorry!" Ava couldn't stop talking. Was this what it was like to be Z? "And I'm really, really sorry I tried to get you and Rodrigo back together too. I was thinking only about myself. I'm not usually bad."

"Making a bad choice and being bad are not the same, sweet pickle." Jenn caught Ava's eye. "You're not bad, Ava."

Would Jenn change her mind, though, if she learned Ava had disabled her Jeep?

"Dad and I had a big talk last night," Ava said. "We're trying to work out some things."

She wasn't sure how much to share, but Jenn looked as if she were listening with her whole, big heart. "He's scared of being a dad," she continued. "I mean, a bad dad."

"He's a fantastic dad."

Ava swallowed. "Are you…did you break up?"

A heavy ache filled Ava's chest. What if she didn't see Jenn again?

"We're trying to work through some things too," Jenn said. "But no matter what happens with your dad and me, Ava, this baby is going to need you."

"Really?"

"Absolutely."

The baby needed her. Ava would see Jenn and Z again, and the baby. No matter what.

"Why didn't you tell Dad you were pregnant?"

"Yeah." Jenn shook her head slightly. "I wanted to tell him in person. Since this whole vacation was for the four of us, a chance to get to know each other and have fun, I couldn't seem to find a good time." She tightened her ponytail. "I should have told you—and sooner. I'm sorry."

Ava nodded as a strange thought occurred to her. Maybe Jenn had been afraid to tell them? Because: The baby—who wasn't born yet—changed everything, for all of them, forever.

"Jenn?" An exciting idea stirred in Ava. "Is it hard—or expensive—to get a watch fixed?"

———

They retrieved their things from the bathhouse locker and threw away Jenn's spoiled sandwich. No one talked as they crossed the parking lot.

In the backseat, Ava practiced slow, deep yoga breaths. She hadn't gotten a chance to say goodbye to José. She hoped she wasn't leaving.

Dad turned to Ava and Z. "Everybody buckled up?"

Z's foot jiggled. "Want some?" She handed Ava a piece of gum. "Thanks." It tasted more chemical than grape. But Ava was grateful. Working her jaw gave her something to do. Plus: Z loved her gum. She wouldn't share with just anybody.

Out of the corner of her eye, something moved. Ava turned to the window and caught her breath. Two ground squirrels—two!—stood on hind legs, revealing cottony white bellies. They craned their necks, their black-seed eyes searching, as if trying to peer into the car.

Ava took another breath. They wanted food. There was nothing to fear. Because: Even if fleas had infected those ground squirrels with plague, and even if those now plague-y ground squirrels bit Ava or someone she loved, they still had a 50 percent chance of survival. And that was without seeing a doctor, which they definitely, for sure would. Obviously.

Jenn started the car. It sounded eager to whisk them off to Denver.

The ground squirrels scampered away. Ava slumped.

The Jeep's engine died.

Z stilled. Ava held her breath.

Jenn restarted the car.

It died again.

"Are you kidding me?" Jenn grumbled, turning the key. Again, the engine whirred to life only to stop a moment later.

It was exactly like the video. They'd done it! Ava, Z, and Dad had kept the Jeep from starting. Now, Dad would find a way to talk to Jenn and make up.

When the Jeep died the third time, Jenn slumped over the steering wheel and cried.

Ava rushed to release her seat belt. "I did it," she shouted, rising from her seat.

"Ava!" Z shouted. "No!"

Ava shook her off. "I'm so sorry, Jenn!" Ava leaned over the front seat, her hand on Jenn's shoulder. "Please don't cry!"

Jenn stared at Ava, then at Dad, whose head was bowed.

"What's going on?" Jenn's voice was low.

"We want to stay, Mom." Z's voice wobbled, and she joined Ava, leaning into the front seat. "Can we please stay?"

Dad placed the plastic fuse in Jenn's palm.

"It's your fuel pump fuse," Ava said. "I—I took it."

"From my car?"

"We want to stay," Dad said. The sun struck a piece of glitter stuck above his eyebrow. "Together."

Jenn's eyes widened. "You knew?"

"It won't hurt the car," he said. "I—"

"I'm sorry." Ava interrupted, her voice barely a whisper. "We… we wanted to stay." She stared at her hands, the floor, anywhere but Jenn's sad, confused face.

"Ava." Jenn gently raised Ava's chin, forcing Ava to meet her eyes. "You want to stay in the mountains? In Colorado?"

"I want to stay with you," Ava said. Jenn's face blurred. "Maybe you can work things out with Dad?"

"Sweet pickle." Jenn hugged Ava and Z, and Dad wrapped his arms around all of them.

Ava closed her eyes. Her heart felt warm and full and good. The rest of her felt almost weightless, strangely open, expansive, and sparkly, like an astronaut freed from gravity.

The four of them together felt right. Like a family. A family of four soon to be five.

Ava felt happy.

No.

Happy happy.

What I'll Miss Most about Iowa

- Grandmom, Granddad, Uncle Steve, Mrs. Mendez, Kylie, Emma, Kylie's mom
- Our little house and big yard
- Grandmom's pond
- Our cows
- Lightning bugs
- Ms. Weber, town librarian
- Mrs. Riccelli, Hillaker Elementary librarian
- Sweet corn, face-sized pork tenderloins, Maid-Rites, walking tacos, Snickers "salad"
- Shorty's hot fudge sundaes
- Telling a joke at Halloween to get candy (What's brown and sticky?*)
- Cheering for the Iowa State Cyclones
- The Iowa State Fair
- Green rolling fields
- Tractor rides
- Waving at people in pickups

* A stick!

Good Things about Moving to Colorado

- No sticky humidity
- 300+ days of sunshine a year
- Bluer skies
- Soaring Eagle Resort
- Burritos with green chili, Palisade peaches, bison burgers, Kettle Head popcorn—Denver Cheddar
- Ice cream shops to try: High Point Creamery, Little Man, Bonnie Brae, Sweet Action
- Tons of bookstores!!!!
- Lots of dog friends for Mouse
- The Rockies—the mountains and the baseball team
- Dad said I can get a phone!!!!!
- Rodrigo is taking us to a concert at Red Rocks!!!
- Z is going to dye my hair a fun color (Dad doesn't know)
- Future baby sibling
- Jenn
- Z—my friend, my sister

ACKNOWLEDGMENTS

I didn't know Jean Reidy when I walked into her home with my laptop and chocolate. Melanie Crowder had invited me to Jean's write-in, but I didn't know her either. (We'd attended the same graduate program at different times.) After living in Iowa for about one hundred years, I'd moved to Colorado. I knew no one. But the women at Jean's—kidlit folks, too—welcomed me. They, and so many others, helped make this book possible. I'm eternally grateful:

To my friends, whose support keeps me going. To the Society of Children's Book Writers and Illustrators, especially the Iowa and Rocky Mountain chapters. To Vermont College of Fine Arts, particularly my advisors: Sharon Darrow, Tim Wynne-Jones, Cynthia Leitich Smith, and Margaret Bechard. To Vermont Studio Center for a scholarship and monthlong residency where I nearly completed the first revision (a speed record for me).

To Jenny Goebel for wise advice. To Alison Preston for "therapy." To Lianna Nielsen, who said "finish your novel" instead of "eat more salads" at our first health-coaching session. To Connie Solera, who improved my writing by teaching me painting. To my ROARS: Dori Hillestad Butler, Wendy Henrichs, and Sarah Mullen Gilbert for having my back. SMG lives in Iowa's real "little house on the dairy" and loaned me her clever name.

To Erika Gonzalez, who generously translated José Martí's poem and corrected my Spanish. To those who patiently helped with facts: Andrea Bobotis donned her moisture-wicking bonnet to review everything yoga; EMS Supervisor Sean Fontaine explained paramedic procedures; SMG (again!) corrected cow-related errors; and video-star mechanic Daniel Jaeger taught me everything I know about fuel pump fuses. To early readers: Hilari Bell, Jane Bigelow, Ceil Boyles, Anna-Maria Crum (who gave me a great title), Laura K. Deal (who taught me the finger-wiggling trick for mountain motion sickness), Claudia Cangilla McAdam, Cheryl Reifsnyder, Christine Riccelli, Denise Vega (whose Believe scholarship sent me to my first RMC-SCBWI conference), and Doug Weber.

To my Critters: Coral Jenrette, Oz Spies, Samantha Cohoe, and Derek Reiner, for friendship, feedback, and tough love. You've made Denver home. Extra monkeys to Coral, who read last-minute chapters and made this book funnier.

To Jacqui Lipton and everyone at Raven Quill Literary Agency for fostering such a positive creative nest. To Andrea Hall for buying the manuscript and everyone at Albert Whitman for your dedicated excellence. To Jon "it's T-shirt" Westmark and Josh "awesomesauce" Gregory for *a-ma-zing* edits; Aphelandra for stunning design (and so much ground squirrel love!); Simini Blocker for wonderful jacket art; and Lisa White and Kiki Schotanus for working so hard to spread the word.

To my agent Kelly Dyksterhouse and my editor Nivair "Dragon Lightning" Gabriel—holy guacamole—you two are the double-rainbow God wink! Thank you *a lot a lot* for making Ava's story richer and the process joyful.

To my late grandparents, who could tell a *story*, y'all! To Jane and Richard Carter, who made me a reader. To the Webers: Abigail for teaching me, Doug for infectious enthusiasm, and Janea for wisdom, humor, and gifs. To Matt Crocker for constant encouragement—C'MON! I used to joke that you'd be a teenager by the time I published a novel. At least you're still a ways from 30!

To Mike Crocker, who makes me laugh every day, especially at myself. A Thunderbird toast to our thirtieth wedding anniversary *next month*—how about thirty more? This book wouldn't exist without my dear friend Sarah Aronson, who encouraged me to play on the page after I'd moved to Denver and forgotten how.